BLACK TYPE

By Kevin Outlaw

Published by Hartley Publications
P.O. Box 100, Devizes, Wiltshire, SN10 4TE

Copyright © 2003

The right of Kevin Outlaw to be identified as the Author of the work has been asserted by him in accordance with the Copyright, Designs and Patents Act 1988.

FIRST EDITION: 2003

All rights reserved. No part of this publication may be reproduced, stored in a retrieval system, or transmitted, in any form or by any means without the prior written permission of the publisher, nor be otherwise circulated in any form of binding or cover other than that in which it is published and without a similar condition being imposed on the subsequent purchaser.

All characters in this publication are fictitious and any resemblance to real persons, living or dead, is purely coincidental.

Acknowledgements:
Dan Bailey, David Clark, Sue Hart, James Pithic.

ISBN: 187331308X

Typeset and make-up by Wentrow Media.
Printed by Elite Colour Print.

For Margaret and Geoff.
Thanks.

Chapter One

In the end, Nathan had known he was in danger, of course he had, how else could he explain why he had employed Christian's security team to shadow his every move? But even so, . . Even so, he never realised - at least, not until the point when he was shot - the lengths to which somebody was prepared to go to snuff out his existence. He had never allowed himself to believe this was anything anywhere near that serious.

It didn't seem conceivable, especially not here. Not here, in a perfectly ordinary train station, drinking coffee from a paper cup and reading the Gazette, waiting for a train that had already been delayed twice. Not in this place, where tangy voices warbled over the speakers and minimum-wage slaves tapped their feet and their watches, as if to make sure they were both still working. Not here, in the world outside of the movies, where people worked mundane nine-to-five jobs, bitched about their boss, played football at weekends, threw away a week's wages on a dead cert', got overlooked for promotion, and never, never, got shot. This was, after all, the real world, and things like this didn't happen in the real world.

Even as he lay there, bleeding to death, he couldn't convince himself otherwise. Even as those last few moments of his life, those precious seconds, played back in his head, skittering like an old tape recording, he couldn't let himself believe it. He was dying, not on the racetrack, where he had always believed he would go, but here, in a dirty train station beneath the careful observation of some highly-paid security personnel and a gangly young porter with a bad case of acne. Here where, if we were to turn the clock back only ten minutes, Nathan had purchased a newspaper. . .

'Just the Gazette, is it, Boss?'

Nathan smiled at the kiosk salesman. 'Thanks.'

He had no idea why he was doing this to himself. He already knew what the papers were saying about his old ride, Tiffany's Toast. The same damned things they had been saying when Nathan was still a jockey.

'That's fifty pence then, Boss.'

Nathan snatched the paper with trembling fingers. 'Keep the change.'

The salesman, a typically robust, unshaven individual who looked like he could do with the extra money, nodded his thanks. Nathan flicked through to the centre pages of the Gazette. Around him, the train station bustled agitatedly, commuters bouncing against each other as they changed platforms. People shouted into their mobile phones, desperately trying to make their wives or their girlfriends or their mistresses understand they would be late because of the bloody state of the railway system. Three Japanese tourists, dripping with hi-tech camera equipment, backpacks and carryalls, quarrelled among themselves, occasionally jabbing condemning fingers at a huge map of Britain. It was not totally inconceivable that one of those tourists would attempt to kill Nathan within the next few minutes.

Two tall men in black suits and designer sunglasses watched from a nearby bench. Security officers. Nathan did his very best to act like he didn't know they were there.

In the Gazette, page thirty-three: Today's prices. Tiff' had the nap. Tiff', ridden by Neil Jacobson, trained by Glen Lampar, owned by Lady Cavanaugh. A horse that would have amounted to nothing without Nathan.

His frozen smile shattered.

The horse was running in the two-thirty at Ascot. Some of the opposition were marked up as fifty-to-one. Nathan knew well enough those prices were nearer hundreds. Only Tiff' was standing out as a horse with the stamina to keep it together. Still, he had known that.

So had somebody else.

And perhaps that was what this - his shattered leg and the late night visitors - was about. Even knowing what he knew now, that somebody was still hunting him, perhaps all this was really about was a misplaced bet.

He winced as he turned back to the kiosk, his lame knee throbbing violently. The salesman was watching him thoughtfully.

'You know who I am, don't you?' Nathan asked.

The salesman, whose nametag announced 'Joseph, ask me for help', leaned forwards, a low animal cunning glimmering in his pinpoint eyes. His doughy face folded into a mirthless smile. 'Must be difficult, watching someone else ride her, Mr O'Donnell.'

Something in that look. Something uncomfortable.

Something that screamed for Nathan to go, to get away from there.

Nathan glanced at the bench. One of the suits - one of his newly appointed bodyguards - had disappeared. The remaining suit was holding two paper cups, from which steady curls of steam were rising. 'There'll be other races,' Nathan said, fully aware he would never ride again. Not in this lifetime.

His quick gaze darted around the milling crowds. Where was the second bodyguard, Christian?

He turned back to Joseph Ask Me For Help, folding his Gazette. 'Thanks again,' he said.

'Any chance of a signa. . .' Joseph watched Nathan's back as the jockey hobbled away. On the bench, the remaining bodyguard waited with coffee in hand. The tip of Nathan's brass-topped cane clattered on the platform, tapping out each painfully obvious step. 'I'll take that as a no, then,' Joseph said.

Over the speakers, another announcement was made. We regret to announce et cetera et cetera. A universal groan escaped the heaving, sweating crowd. There was the shimmer of silver mobile phones re-emerging from jacket pockets. Yes, he would be late. No, hold all his calls. Yes, if his wife phones, he's fine. Make sure the children get picked up from school. Feed the dog. And so on and so on and so on.

Nathan collapsed on the bench next to the suit, gratefully accepting the paper cup thrust unceremoniously in his face. 'This isn't decaffeinated, is it?' he asked. The suit shrugged.

Nathan sampled the coffee. Damned if he could tell whether it was decaf' or not, barely even tasted like coffee. Several minutes silently made their escape. The world rolled by.

'Any sign of them yet?' he risked.

The bodyguard - Carl - shook his head, clearly bored. Nathan tried to read the front page of the newspaper, but the hiss and squeal of trains arriving at other platforms was a persistent source of annoyance, reminding him his train had been delayed by twenty minutes already. Nobody else seemed to be having any problems. Somehow, it always seemed to be that way.

He gulped his coffee. Carl slurped his. Nathan wondered whether anybody nurtured the art of conversation anymore when they weren't on the phone.

'Nothing unusual at all?' he tried.

'No.'

Nathan, deciding a monosyllabic response was about the best he could hope for, turned his attention back to the paper.

Nobody, it appeared, would be paying him a visit. Not today.

Of course, he hadn't really expected anybody to show. Last night, perhaps he thought differently, but it was so much easier to dismiss Christian's theories in the light of day. In the light of day, the letters were just that: letters. In the light of day, his stalker - or stalkers - was some crank enjoying ruffling a few feathers. That was all.

Okay, so he had employed the services of some bodyguards, but that was just sensible. He was a star, it was wise to have a little muscle around. He had never really believed somebody was going to hunt him down and kill him, despite Christian's dark warnings. Despite the face at his window the previous night.

If something was going to happen, it would have happened by now. If somebody wanted him out of the race today, they had succeeded. If it was all nothing more than a matter of coincidence, then that was fine too. Nobody was gunning for him.

He opened the Gazette.

Of course nobody was going to try killing him. This was the real world. . .

But that had been ten minutes ago.

He started reading an article on street crime. Children were at increased risk from thugs looking to steal mobile phones. He seemed to remember thinking crime was as alien to him as Mars, something which, until recently, he had only ever read about in books. Now, as the shadow of his assassin - for it could only be his assassin - fell across him, he was living his own book. He knew instinctively - and it was nothing to do with what had happened at the racecourse, or the letters he had been receiving - that tomorrow morning, he would be the story in the Gazette. Crazily, incomprehensibly, the words floated into his mind as he looked up at the cold, dark eyes of his killer. 'I don't even have a mobile phone anymore.'

He had always imagined his dying words would be somewhat more prophetic.

The muzzle of the silenced nine millimetre handgun trembled only slightly, then flashed. There was a dull whump. Nathan's newspaper disintegrated in a flutter of black and white teeth. Something solid and warm slammed against his chest.

But this was the real world and things like this didn't happen, couldn't happen, in the real world. He told himself that as he tumbled forwards, a terrible, sickening warmth already spreading outwards from the alien slug lodged between his ribs.

He hit the slabs of the train station platform, saw the handgun flare and jump again in his assassin's hand. He was being shot again. Didn't even feel the second impact, already too far gone by then, already slipping through the layers of reality. Only aware of the figure crouching silently next to him.

He tried to cry out for help, but too late.

Too late.

Nathan was already dead.

Chapter Two

Of course, this wasn't the first time Nathan had died, although it was unquestionably the last. Considering the number of people he hurt, in the months preceding the ultimate end of his existence, two deaths didn't seem at all bad.

There is, however, always a point when the rot sets in. The problem is, finding out exactly when.

Perhaps it was the morning of what would eventually turn out to be Nathan's very last race. A non-too-serious chase over fences at Chepstow on a horse that was three legs shy of the glue factory.

Perhaps it was the first time he received a death threat; huge, black characters cut out of newspaper type and glued to unbranded, widely-available copier paper.

Or perhaps even that was jumping the gun. Maybe it started when he impressed Lampar by leading Tiffany's Toast out over a slightly longer distance, taking a first in an extremely competitive field, thrusting himself and the horse into the limelight and earning the right to first refusal on all Tiff's future outings. Before the bad things started to happen.

Before the gunshots, the tatters of newspaper headlines. Long before Nathan ever knew what it was to be afraid. . .

*

Early morning, almost five o'clock, and the best part of the day was stretching out before Nathan like a well-worn footpath.

He was still in a towelling robe at that time, wearing a pair of novelty football shaped slippers his imaginative cousin had bought him for Christmas and studying his tired expression in the mirror. He had often thought that for a twenty-five year old man he did a pretty good impression of a forty year old but, never-the-less, he was handsome, and at least one hour of personal grooming each day went some way towards defying the dramatic ageing process of his chosen career.

With a large mug of steaming coffee close to hand he went about the daily rituals of shaving to avoid the discomfort of a helmet strap tightened across stubble and pampering himself with a series of spells and potions recommended to him by a rather attractive woman in the chemist, whose number he had received, and who he had yet to call, despite meaning to do so. Only then would he allow himself to sit down to a breakfast of dry toast and a cigarette. With no racing scheduled for the day, and no dreaded weigh in, he also treated himself to a soft-boiled egg.

It was only six-thirty by the time he was ready to leave the house, still dark, but he couldn't allow the woman in his bed to stay there, so he woke her anyway.

'Hey,' he said, poking her.

There were inarticulate noises from the bundle of duvet.

'Hey, come on. Time to get up.' He shook her this time, and like a turtle emerging from its shell, a bleary-eyed, makeup-streaked face popped out at him through the crumpled sheets. He supposed, though he wasn't entirely sure, she had looked better than this last night. He certainly hoped so. 'I have to go to the office,' he said.

The face looked confused, then smiled. There was a lot of residual vodka in that smile, and the smell of it was almost overpowering when the girl - only a girl, perhaps seventeen - spoke. 'You don't have an office.'

'I know. . .' Damn it, her name was on the tip of his tongue but he couldn't quite spit it out. 'I mean I have to go across to the stables.'

'I thought you weren't racing today,' she said, sitting up. He had to admit, even with the panda-like makeup, the smell of alcohol and the less than attractive crust of vomit on her bottom lip, she had a certain quality. Still couldn't remember her name though. Made it difficult to phone.

'No races,' he said, sitting on the edge of the bed, slightly turned away from her to avoid a full-on assault of the senses by the stench of vodka, 'but that doesn't mean I have the day off.'

'Can't you take the day off?'

'Why?' The question was asked honestly enough. He could think of no valid reason why he should want to spend any more time with this girl.

'I thought,' she gestured uselessly with her hands. 'You know. That we might do something.'

Nathan sneered. 'Like, hang out? Do stuff?'

'Yeah.'

'How old are you?'

The girl, nameless and beautiful, looked down at her hands as they worried each other. 'I told you last night. I'm eighteen.'

'Sorry?'

'Eighteen.'

'In dog years?'

Her head snapped up. Amazing how quickly the alcohol can swim out of a person's eyes when there is the flare of anger to replace it. 'I'm eighteen.'

'And I'm the pope.' He stood, caught a quick glimmer of his reflection in the mirror. He was fully clothed now, in workable trousers and a smart roll-neck sweater. He was wearing a breast cancer awareness pin, which was entirely for the benefit of any attractive girls in doubt as to whether he was as caring as he claimed to be. 'Anyway, I have to go. That means you have to go.'

'Can't I just. . ?' She looked at him with large, pleading eyes. She seemed to be getting younger by the second. What if she wasn't eighteen? What if she wasn't even sixteen? What if. . ?

'No,' he said, flatly. 'I can't let you stay here unattended. We're on the stable grounds, it isn't allowed.' He silently cursed himself. Why hadn't they gone back to her place? He knew the answer to that. She was just a kid. She was living with her parents.

Damn.

She pulled the duvet closer around her shoulders, but left just enough of her leg visible to be persuasive. Young, yes, but not anywhere near as dumb as he had thought. 'I thought this was your place,' she said. 'Surely I can stay here.'

'No,' he repeated. 'The cottage is part of the agreement I have with the Governor. If I leave you here and then you go off feeding sugar lumps to the horses my ass is on the line.'

'I'll stay here until you get back.'

'You'll go now.'

The girl - Christ, what was her name? - sighed heavily. 'Okay,' she relented. 'But will you call me sometime?'

'Course,' Nathan said as kindly as he could, well aware he didn't have her phone number. 'I'll leave you to get dressed.'

He backed out of the room, returned to the kitchen. The day was still dark, waiting the bright paint strokes of the sun.

He smoked a cigarette. He had smoked three more by the time the girl came down the stairs, wearing the red, low-cut dress she had been wearing at the party last night. His coffee mug was empty.

'You need a lift anywhere?' he asked.

'No,' she said. Without asking, she tapped a cigarette from Nathan's pack. 'I suppose you'll need to walk me off the premises though.'

'Of course.'

'Make sure I haven't got any sugar lumps on me?'

'Something like that.'

She looked defeated. She knew she had been used. She was taking it admirably well.

She sat on the edge of the kitchen table and lit the cigarette. In complete silence she smoked it right down to the orange butt, blowing smoke at the ceiling. The designer slash up the left of her dress revealed just enough thigh to make Nathan need to turn away. The first rays of daylight began to flicker on the horizon.

'Ready?' Nathan asked, when the girl finally stubbed out the cigarette.

The girl, who had removed the remnants of her smeared makeup to reveal an extremely attractive face - the kind of face that didn't even need makeup - nodded. 'I guess so.'

Nathan stood, relieved. Ugly moment was over.

'I was just wondering, though,' she said, watching him slyly. 'Why did you pick me?'

He winced, considered the most appropriate response. 'Because you're beautiful.'

'There were other beautiful people there.'

Nathan dredged the sludgy waters of his memory. The Jockey's Fund dance had been as glittering and polished as it always was. That was the problem. All those oh-so-proper people eating oh-so-proper finger buffet foods and drinking oh-so-proper champagne until their oh-so-proper sentences were unrecognisably slurred. Indeed, there had been beautiful people there, and handsomely rich people, and powerfully conceited people. Nathan had no interest in any of them. He had been interested in only one person. A beautifully innocent person. Someone who would be grateful in the morning, even after he kicked her out. His self-assured grin broadened.

'There was nobody like you,' he said. 'Now let me give you that lift.'

'All the way home?'

'The least I can do.'

Condensation twinkled on the kitchen windows, spangling the walls with droplets of refracted sunlight. It was going to be a wonderful day.

'You're right,' the girl said. 'But are you sure it's wise?'

Nathan grabbed a jacket from its hook in the hallway. 'Why wouldn't it be?'

'Last I heard, you didn't exactly get on too well with Mr Corelli.'

Nathan's eyes widened at the mere mention of the old trainer's name. There was a sudden rush of blood thundering between his ears, his heart bucked. 'Don't tell me you're his daughter,' he said.

'Just one of his stable lasses. I live at the stables.' Her smile was sharp as a knife, dripping with poison. 'Oops. Didn't I mention that before?'

'I guess not,' Nathan said, matching her smile with an uneasy one of his own.

'Still want to give me that lift?'

He thought about it. 'Okay. It's not like I have to meet him, is it?'

'Of course not.'

'And it's been a long time since I was at the stables.' He laughed uncomfortably. 'Maybe not quite long enough.'

From where it had been thrown over the back of a kitchen chair, he took the girl's coat and waved it at her, making no move to help her put it on. She snatched it out of his hand and wriggled her arms into the sleeves. 'He still talks about you sometimes,' she said.

'I'm touched,' Nathan said, throwing on his jacket and jangling his car keys loud enough to make the point. End of conversation. Time to go.

'He says he'll never forgive you.' She paused, just long enough to gauge where the fine line was. 'Of course, he doesn't say that to me. But you hear things. Sometimes you hear more than you'd like to.'

'Really?' Nathan raised an eyebrow questioningly. 'Like what?'

She breezed past him, grabbing his car keys. 'I'll drive.'

'Like what?'

'Oh, this and that.' She ran out of the front door and dashed down the gravel driveway towards his awaiting Jag'. Nathan followed casually.

'Like what?' he repeated. She already had the car door open, but that was as far as she got before he wrestled the key from her grasp and directed her to the passenger seat.

'Things about you,' she said.

'So I gather, but what sort of things?'

She pondered the question for a moment, decided to ignore it. 'What was it that happened between you two?'

'Never answer a question with a question.'

She stuck her tongue out, he fired up the Jag'. The well-maintained car thrummed comfortably as he backed out of the drive and turned towards the main gates of the stable. He was due out on the gallops in an hour, if he made this quick, he might not be too late.

They drove in silence for the whole journey, Nathan occasionally glaring at the girl as she drifted in and out of a restless sleep beside him, and it was not until he pulled in at the gates to Barrowdown, the small stables Corelli had founded, that he made any effort to strike up further conversation.

'Last stop,' he said.

In the early-morning mist, the gloomy manor house owned by Nathan's old Governor stood out stark and black, an incredible fiend encompassed by trees like withered claws. The grounds stretched out in undulating waves of brown-green grass. Rutted paths and tracks marked the regular passage of Land Rovers and horse boxes. A row of stable blocks trailed off towards a fenced enclosure to the north. There were no immediate signs of activity.

Nathan glanced at the girl. She was dozing. 'Hey, wake up.' He gave her a shove and she snapped awake. 'Time for you to go.'

Wide fingers of sunlight crept up behind the house like the legs of a giant spider. The mist was a delicate web, coiling tighter around the silent landscape. Nathan shivered.

'Thanks for the lift,' the girl said, getting out of the car and buttoning her jacket. 'I suppose you best get out of here before someone sees you.'

'I suppose so.'

The girl hesitated for a moment, looking across the stable grounds at nothing in particular. The sun struggled to illuminate her surroundings, but here it was destined to remain grey and wet for several hours to come. 'It's Nina,' she said.

Nathan's brow creased with puzzlement. 'Sorry?'

'My name. It's Nina.'

'I was wondering.'

'I know.'

'How could you tell?'

'Lucky guess. You aren't going to phone me either, are you?'

He sucked his teeth thoughtfully. 'Maybe it isn't such a good idea.'

'Maybe not.' The mist spiralled and zig-zagged around her. A light came on in one of the upstairs windows of the house. Life. 'It's worse than you realise,' she said, wrapping her arms across her chest. There was more than the chill of mist in the air.

'What is?'

'Corelli. He's losing his business.' She smiled meekly. 'He's losing everything.'

Nathan looked from Nina to the house, then out at the ranks of empty stables. He had heard rumours, of course he had, the dance the previous evening had been swimming with them. Did you hear? Had you heard? They couldn't be true though. For everything else he might have been, Corelli was a good trainer. He lacked any kind of vision, but he was good. At least, he had been.

'I'm sorry to hear that,' Nathan said, surprised to realise he actually was. 'But it doesn't have anything to do with me.'

Nina wrapped her arms more tightly across her chest as if to form a barrier between herself and the cruelty of the world. Her breath plumed elegantly in the vaporous mist. 'I wouldn't bet on it,' she said.

Chapter Three

Nathan arrived back at Zephyr Fields Stables at nine thirty and, as he always did when he was late, pretended like he had been there all morning. As always, this didn't work, but as a rider of some considerable talent, certain exceptions were made.

The Governor, Mr Glen Lampar, a jovial individual with a good deal more interest in malt whiskey and beautiful ladies than he had ever exhibited for horses, was sitting in the forecourt of the manor house smoking a cigarette and sucking on a hip flask. His face, a ruddy, fat mask of feigned sobriety, was twisted with the kinds of thoughts he usually paid other people to have for him.

Nathan sat opposite, drawing heavily on his own cigarette.

'Where have you been?' Lampar asked. His almost complete lack of interest in whatever the response might be would have been disconcerting to most. Nathan took it all in his stride.

'Here.'

'You lie like my mother.'

'I am your mother.'

'Can't be. You're prettier.'

'You're far too drunk for this time of day.'

Lampar chuckled, fingered his hip flask thoughtfully, then upended the contents down his throat. 'You missed Tiffany's Toast doing some work. Fine young horse. One of the best.' There was more whiskey in his voice than there was conviction.

Nathan waited to see if there was any more to come. There wasn't and he was forced to fill the encroaching silence with something that he hoped was upbeat. 'She's a star.'

'She's a star.' Lampar's gaze was distant and not altogether focussed on anything in particular. 'You should have seen her this morning.'

'I had other matters to attend to.'

'With that girl?'

Nathan smiled. Lampar had been at the Jockey's Fund dance as well; of course he had seen the girl. 'Nina. Nice kid.'

'You said it.'

'Said what?'

'Kid.'

Nathan glanced at the sun-glazed horizon, pictured the girl's face. The face he had seen once the makeup had come off, when she had stopped being the girl with the panda-black eyes. When she had allowed herself to be seen for what she really was.

For a moment something inside Nathan crumbled, almost snapped beneath an absurd and undisclosed weight. He chose to ignore it.

The stables were strangely peaceful, awaiting some menace.

'You shouldn't be wasting your time running around after her sort,' Lampar slurred.

'I couldn't just leave her here, Boss.'

Lampar sat back, letting his heavy eyelids flutter closed. Deep, red veins criss-crossed his cheeks and nose like a road map. 'She works for Corelli,' he said. His voice was calm but the statement was clearly an accusation.

'You never mentioned that last night.'

'Would you have cared?'

'I doubt it.'

'So what would have been the point?' His eyes came open again and Nathan could see they were no more than tiny red pinpricks in fleshy white pits. The last year, and the alcohol, had been unkind on the old trainer. This nonsense with Tiff' and her owners wasn't helping matters.

Nathan sucked smoke into his lungs, savouring the bitter-sweet contraction. 'She tells me the rumours about Corelli may not be too far from the truth.'

'That so?'

'Says he's losing the lot.'

Lampar carefully - too carefully - screwed the lid back on his hip flask and, on the second attempt, pocketed it. 'How do you feel about that?' he asked.

'Not sure.'

'Do you care?'

'Not enough to throw him a lifeline, if that's what you're thinking.'

'I have a contract that says you can't, but the question is, do you want to?'

'You know there are bad things between Corelli and I. I can't help him get out of this one.'

'Even though you may be the one that put him there in the first place?' Lampar let a thick laugh rumble in his throat. The alcohol had dulled his wits but not, it would appear, his tongue.

'I didn't do anything I wasn't within my rights to do. This is a tough business.'

'And you're a tough son-of-a-bitch.'

Nathan crunched his cigarette under the heel of one shoe. It hissed pleasantly as he ground it to pulp. 'I most certainly am,' he said.

'Still, some people might say you didn't do the right thing.'

'Some people weren't in the situation I was in. He didn't leave me a lot of options.'

'And yet here you are, working for me, nice car, nice house, while Corelli's business evaporates up its own posterior.' He leaned closer. 'A lot of people wouldn't understand that.'

Nathan shook his head. 'You understand, Boss. I guess that's good enough.'

'I understand, but what if it happened again. Would you do the same thing to me you did to that poor sap?'

'Of course.'

Lampar frowned, then caught the twinkle in Nathan's eye. 'You're a good boy, Nathan. Honest.'

'To a fault,' Nathan lied.

'But maybe you shouldn't go bringing girls back here for a while.'

Lampar cleared his throat. 'At least, not girls from a stable run by a well-known loser on the verge of a complete mental breakdown.'

'Understood, Boss.' Nathan fished out a fresh cigarette and lit it. The flame of his lighter whipped and danced sporadically. 'Why don't you tell me what I've missed this morning?'

'I think you know.'

'I've seen Tiff' run before, Boss. It isn't the end of the world.'

'Tiff's your ride, our biggest asset. You should care about that.'

'I do, but I don't see the point in showing when you insist on running her short.'

'Haven't we already discussed this?' The tiredness was clear in Lampar's voice. Nathan wondered how far he could push him.

'Of course.'

'Then you know what a complete,' Lampar leaned even closer, clapping Nathan on the shoulder. The whiskey on his breath was enough to make Nathan's eyes water. 'What a complete b - i - t - c - h that woman can be.'

Nathan knew well enough. The b - i - t - c - h in question was no less than Lady Cavanaugh, Lord Cavanaugh's third wife, recently pulled feet first out of the gutter and still talking a lot of the rubbish she had been brought up in. Her new-money status was as obvious as a flashing neon sign, evident in her gaudy jewellery and excessive dresses. Nathan had rarely had cause to dislike somebody so much, but when she had called him 'lad' the last time she had come around to the stables she had earned herself his enduring hatred.

He masked all those feelings behind his perfect, rather dashing, smile.

'The Cavanaugh's want the horse to win, Boss. I think it can.'

Lampar glanced across to the stable block where a line of fresh young faces were leading out the second string of the day. There were some good horses in that lot, a few resting, a few not quite fit enough, but there wasn't one there that had ever been as promising as Tiffany's Toast. If only he could be allowed a free reign over what to do with the bloody animal.

The stable hands trudged by, some of them shooting Nathan a paint-stripping look when they were certain he wasn't paying attention. Their booted feet drummed out the rhythm of the stable's heartbeat. The sun had burned away all but the last of the mist.

'Tiff' can win,' Lampar said. 'Of course she can. But I don't have the last call.

'You're the trainer. You always have the last call.' Nathan watched the horses disappearing into a beaten path through hawthorn bushes leading out to the all-weather gallops. 'And if you don't, you should take steps to ensure you do.'

'You think you could do better?' Lampar snorted a laugh through his nose that sounded sickeningly like it had dislodged something better left lodged.

'I think so, yes.'

There was enough calculated assurance in Nathan's grin to make Lampar believe him.

The sun flickered and strobed as it rose up above the trees where robins flitted and bobbed theatrically. The elongated shadow of a rapidly moving, gangly young man attired in a less-than-suitable dinner suit, bobbed towards them across the gravel yard. As he approached he waved enthusiastically.

'You can start right now,' Lampar said, with a devilish grin.

'Christ. Lady Cavanaugh's son? You never said he was here.'

'Why else would I be drinking at nine-thirty in the morning?'

'When did he arrive?'

'Before you. One of the lads saw him hanging around first thing. Do you think he'd notice if I just slipped off?'

The youth, now within twenty paces and still accelerating, was wiping his hands in the back of his trousers in a custom that suggested he would be wanting to shake hands with someone.

'Why is he dressed like that?' Nathan whispered. Lampar shrugged.

Then the youth was standing over them, flustered with excitement, an ungainly mop of black hair flapping around his shoulders as he looked this way and that with the wide-eyed anticipation of a child on Christmas morning. One would be inclined to believe this was his first venture to the stables.

'Morning, Terence,' Nathan said, in a tone that suggested an exclamation of fact more so than a greeting of any kind.

'Mr O'Donnell, Sir.' Terence extended a pale hand which, reluctantly, Nathan accepted. The handshake was as limp as Terence's hair. 'It's a pleasure to meet you again, Sir. I trust you're keeping well.'

'I've been worse. How's your mother?'

'The old battleaxe?' Terence laughed with a callousness that threatened to reveal how little he actually cared for her. 'You know what the lady of the manor can be like.'

'We certainly do,' Lampar said, standing and failing to acknowledge the hand that Terence thrust at him. 'How long have you been on the premises, Son?'

Terence checked his Rolex. 'About half an hour.'

'You may want to let me know the next time.' Lampar clapped him on the shoulder. 'I may think you're a trespasser and have you shot.'

Terence's perpetual grin widened startlingly. 'No problem. And how's Tiff' today?' Perhaps he chose to ignore the serious undertone in Lampar's voice. Perhaps he was just too dumb to tell.

'Restless,' Nathan said.

'Really?'

'We need to have a serious discussion.'

'Sounds terribly ominous.'

Nathan put his arm around Terence's shoulders. 'It is,' he said. 'Terribly.'

*

After five minutes of Terence's bleating and complaining, Glen Lampar had resorted to the only sensible option, retiring to his study with a glass of whiskey and the suddenly-remembered task of organising some meetings with important clients that didn't really exist.

Nathan, having dug his own grave by attempting to reason with a half-wit who, by his own admission, had more bank balance than brain, could make no such cunning escape.

'Be reasonable, Terence.'

They were situated in the dining room of Lampar's habitual residence with as much of the expansive table between them as Nathan could arrange. Here, in the large echoic room where each morning the stable hands gathered to talk about the horses and periodically get bawled out by the Governor, Terence appeared perfectly at home and his reverence for the great Nathan O'Donnell was disappearing as rapidly as the weak sugary tea he was drinking.

From between heavy, red drapes, the sun blinked cautiously. The clunk of statuettes being pushed around by an uncomfortable looking maid with a duster filled the silence during the periods when Terence was thinking rather than talking. Such times were depressingly scarce.

Nathan sipped his coffee and smoked.

'It's my horse,' Terence said, and Nathan was appalled at how childlike he sounded.

'I know it's your horse, nobody's disputing that. But you aren't a trainer, Terence. Lampar knows what the horse needs to win.'

The maid - beautiful, in a plain kind of way - brushed by Nathan's arm.

'I tell you now' - at this point, Terence thumped the table for dramatic impact, possibly something he had seen done in a movie once, although the hero in the movie no doubt looked much more impressive when he did it - 'I'll say how she should be run, not you. When she wins, and mark my words, she will win, I'm going to be the one that gets the credit. Not you. Me.'

Nathan shook his head with dismay, his downcast eyes wreathed by cigarette smoke. He couldn't be having this conversation. Surely nobody, not even the son of the ridiculously outspoken Lady

Cavanaugh, could be so utterly foolish.

'You still get to go and pick up the bloody trophies, Terence. You still get the prestige of owning a damned fine animal. Isn't that enough?'

'Frankly, no.' Nathan watched Terence slurp his tea, secretly hoping the young brat would choke on his silver spoon. Nathan very much doubted it would happen, considering the spoon had long ago been pulled out of Terence's mouth and shoved firmly up his backside.

'Do you want to own a winner or a horse that's never going to make the frame?'

The maid opened the door into the hallway. As she left, she turned back and winked at Nathan. Nathan shot her a grin, wondering whether he had ever slept with her.

'I'm sorry, Mr O'Donnell, but I insist on having the final say on Tiff's outings, and that's all there is to be said on the matter,' Terence whined, displaying a lot more backbone than Nathan had ever believed possible. 'I am the owner, it's my right.'

Nathan sat back in his chair with a heartfelt sigh. Clearly, he was getting nowhere here. 'How old are you, Terence?' The question sounded more condemning than he had intended it to.

'Eighteen.'

'And what do you do?'

'I'm at college.'

'Really? That must be hard work.' He smiled coldly. His contempt for educated fops was only slightly overshadowed by his contempt for rich, stupid ones. 'All that studying. Can't give you much time to do the things you'd like.'

'I find time.'

'And now you have your own racehorse.'

'Indeed.'

'That's very impressive for an eighteen year old still in college.'

'You sound jealous.'

Nathan clenched his hands, bit his lip. 'Why would I be jealous? I get to ride her. Unless, of course, you think you might like to do that in future.'

'Don't be ridiculous.' Terence's face was clouded and thoughtful. He had the impression he was being led into a trap he could not fathom nor escape from. He was almost completely overcome by a terrible sense of impending doom. His mouth twitched cautiously.

'Why's that ridiculous?'

'Because I don't know the first thing about riding a bloody racehorse.'

Nathan's smiled broadened. The trap snapped closed with an almost audible twang. He said nothing.

'But that's completely different,' Terence protested, stirring the dregs of his tea feverishly. 'Riding and training are a world apart.'

'Why don't you tell Mr Lampar that. I'm sure he could find the time to tell you about his twenty years of experience over the fences and how terribly irrelevant it is to his current occupation.'

Terence remained silent, eyes down. Outside, the maid clattered and bashed about, probably dusting the glass she had pressed to the dining room door.

In the courtyard, there was shouting and laughing, the tramping of horses' hooves on compacted soil. 'Do you hear that?' Nathan asked, jerking an uncommonly aggressive thumb at the window.

'Yes.'

'You ever do anything like that?'

'Like what?'

'Exercise some lots, muck out a stable.'

'Muck out?'

'You know. Did you ever pull on a big, old pair of boots and get knee-deep in excrement? Did you ever do for a horse?'

Terence looked almost horrified. 'Of course not.'

'That's what I thought.'

Terence drank the rest of his tea, clattering the cup in its saucer agitatedly. He was unaccustomed to being attacked in this manner, but he was damned if he was going to get up and walk out.

The grandfather clock in the corner of the room ticked monotonously, each passage of its giant pendulum like that of the executioner's axe, chopping hours into sharp, unnatural seconds.

'Eighteen,' Nathan mused, removing the last cigarette from his packet and lighting it. He drank smoke for almost a minute before speaking again. 'Eighteen years old. Seems a little young to actually own a horse.'

'What's your point?'

'Do you actually own the horse?'

'I told you, the horse is mine. Mother gave it to me.'

Nathan raised an eyebrow, planted his feet comfortably on the dining table. 'Indeed, the bountiful Lady Cavanaugh. That was very generous of her. Did she happen to sign over any paperwork to you?'

'Paperwork?'

'A deed of ownership.'

'I guess she must have done.'

'Really? Because I think she just told you the horse was yours but left everything in her name.' His chair rocked back. 'Is that the truth of it, Terence? Is this really your mother's horse?'

'No.' Terence stood impatiently, hands trembling, face screwed up with anger. There was a lot of bruised ego that would need nursing in the near future. 'The horse is mine and I get the final say on her training. If you don't like it, I'll take her elsewhere.'

Nathan nodded solemnly. 'No, Terence. You're right. The horse is yours and you should decide on the races she takes part in.'

Immediately the creases smoothed out of Terence's young face. The anger drained away and was almost instantly replaced with a look of vague superiority. 'I'm glad that's sorted,' he said.

Nathan smashed out his cigarette in a crystal ashtray. 'So am I,' he said.

Chapter Four

Lord Cavanaugh, at seventy-eight years of age, had two things the average man would be envious of. Firstly, he had a gold mine in Africa that turned out just enough profit each year to ensure he, and all of his descendants, would never need to do anything more strenuous than cut steak or crack lobster shells. Secondly, he had a beautiful thirty-six year old wife who was so enamoured by the shiny things he bought for her she hadn't even considered divorcing him yet, despite the fact he was a thoroughly unpleasant individual.

It was the latter of these two things that Nathan was interested in.

The stunning Lady Cavanaugh. A complete bitch with absolutely no scruples and an almost inhuman hunger to have things done her way. Nathan had dealt with her kind on more than one occasion in the past and, while he may have hated her with an almost inhuman passion, he had to admit, she did have her. . . uses.

He took the drive, through land that one could be excused for believing was a public park, steadily. His invitation had been marked for two o'clock. He didn't want to show up until at least two-thirty.

He had phoned Cavanaugh, or Deirdre as he now insisted on calling her, shortly after her adequately appeased son had left the stables crowing - not too loudly - about his great victory. The poor boy had been far too ridiculous to realise the battle hadn't even truly started yet. 'Deirdre,' Nathan had said on the phone, keeping his tone light but not exactly playful. 'We need to have words, Honey. Can I come over?'

She had been almost too shocked to respond at first, but she recovered gracefully, uming and ahing for a suitably decent amount of time before settling on a 'yes' and extending the courtesy to Mr Lampar if he so wished to visit. Nathan was quietly pleased to notice the forced calmness in her voice, and the strained impression of disappointment when he told her that Mr Lampar would be far too busy to attend.

Nathan was only a jockey, ranking, despite his indisputable success, somewhere among the riffraff as far as Deirdre was concerned, but she had taken something of a shine to him. She would, she said, certainly appreciate his 'personal assistance' as an 'expert in the field'.

As he drove, the Jag' reverberating almost silently around him, well-oiled engine throbbing dutifully with the barely suppressed power of many racehorses, he tapped his steering wheel in time to the music pumping out of the radio's speakers. Kate Bush was wailing about Heathcliff and, although he didn't really know the words, Nathan would occasionally burst into a roaring accompaniment. His mood was exuberant, his handling of the situation with the young Master Cavanaugh having already put him in good spirits after a morning he would otherwise rather forget.

A morning with Nina.

Nina, who had not cried. Nina, who had calmly accepted the way she had been used. Nina, who had been drunk and angry and unforgettably beautiful all at the same time. Nina, whose name he had not even been able to recall in the light of day.

He smiled vaguely.

Nina, who had turned over in the night and, with only the faintest of murmurs, put her arm around him.

He rolled the window, allowing a drift of fresh, cool air to bustle into the car. The trees that loomed up on either side of the seemingly never-ending driveway watched with a quiet purpose, gnarly limbs stretching high into a blue-white sky. Crows, like hunched black gargoyles, followed his passage with beady eyes, occasionally croaking a dire welcome and shivering their black feathers with an audible crackling rustle.

'Good afternoon,' Nathan shouted, causing several of the birds to flap and screech. Then suddenly, as if he had passed some kind of initiation, the trees opened up onto a huge garden. No trees here, no crows, only expansive plains of striped grass fringed with high hedgerows.

The driveway, wide enough to be considered a road, cut a true line straight through the garden, effectively creating two distinctive lawns, one of which was designed around a towering water fountain. The naked, totally ostentatious, stone woman, who dribbled water down her chin and formed the centrepiece to the fountain, looked toward the direction of the imposing trees, her frozen glare condemning any intruders in this quiet haven. Just another typically cold woman.

Even in these chilled, barren months before Christmas, the land was beautifully kept and Nathan could well imagine summer cocktail parties out on the lawns. Croquet sets and champagne, lobster and caviar. Just the type of affair he couldn't stand. Just the type of affair he was forced to constantly endure in order to further his career.

A single stereotypical gardener, flat cap and all, watched him pass by.

Nathan waved at the grounds' man as he passed, but all the jockey's attention was taken by the flat, unwelcoming edifice that was the Cavanaugh residence. Giant, arched windows, dark and lifeless, stared down at him as he rolled his car to a halt in the expansive forecourt, parking alongside a sparkling silver Bentley. Black tentacles of ivy twisted up the house walls, choking the life out of its bleached stonework. The place was a brave stronghold, but it had been ravaged by time and half-hearted patchwork repairs were evident around the cornerstones and fascia board. A flag bearing the Cavanaugh family crest - battling eagles over a green sun - snapped in the harsh wind, atop a crumbling tower.

The front doors, metal studded and ripped from the pages of a medieval thriller, were stood ajar, a black suited butler waiting on the porch expectantly, arms folded.

Nathan approached with a bounce in his stride that the butler seemed to take offence to.

'Good afternoon,' Nathan said, offering a hand which was rejected by a casual flick of the butler's head.

'The Lady of the house is waiting for you in the lounge.'

'Lead on, Lurch.'

The butler looked down at Nathan through wire spectacles. 'Indeed. Would Sir require a drink of any kind? Something warm, perhaps?'

Nathan had already shrugged himself out of his jacket, which he thrust into the butler's hand. 'Whiskey would be fine,' he said. 'You can stir it into some black coffee, if you like.' He smiled and the butler forced himself to smile back. 'No sugar.'

'Follow me, Sir.'

The butler, heels clicking in the silence of a house several sizes too large for the number of occupants, led Nathan through the entrance hall, beneath a tinkling crystal chandelier that wrapped the sunlight bouncing through the windows into attractive, wirey designs on the walls.

The two men made their way down a corridor of paintings, a high-ceilinged tunnel that drilled its way through the history of the Cavanaugh dynasty and threw its most interesting characters out on canvas for the casual passer-by to admire. Some of the characters, Nathan deduced, were Italian.

'Nice pad,' he said, his voice echoing.

'Indeed.'

'You worked for the Cavanaughs long?'

The butler shot Nathan a weary look that said more than words. 'Indeed.'

At the end of the corridor, the butler pushed open a door that revealed a large room, dominated on one wall by a crackling open fire set in natural stone. The walls were lined with shelves of books, none of which looked to have been written any time in the last century. At a round coffee table, reclining slightly in a high-backed leather couch with a glass of sherry delicately poised in one hand, a restless Lady Cavanaugh watched Nathan enter.

'I'll bring that drink through for you, Sir,' the butler said.

Nathan nodded politely, without letting his gaze slip away from the quite magnificent sight of Deirdre, legs crossed demurely, delicate blouse undone at the neck just enough to reveal the handsome line of her throat and the beginning of a suitably impressive cleavage. Her dark eyes, fringed by extensively enhanced black lashes, batted, just once, before she spoke.

'You're late, Mr O'Donnell.'

'I know, the drive was longer than expected. Mind if I sit?'

Without waiting for a response, he plumped himself into a brown couch opposite Deirdre, a playful gleam betraying his intent. She caught the look and her hard features melted into a more pleasant expression.

'It's been a long time, Mr O'Donnell.'

'Deirdre, please, call me Nathan. Titles make me nervous.'

'Fine. Nathan, what do you want?'

Nathan let himself slide a little further into the couch. 'You don't beat about the bush, do you, Deirdre?'

'I have neither the time nor inclination for games. I'm a busy lady.'

'I don't doubt it, all those coffee mornings and buffet lunches. All those yachts and dinner dances. So little 'me' time, right?'

Deirdre arranged herself more comfortably in her chair, leaving enough of her shapely legs showing beneath the fringe of an overly-detailed skirt to keep Nathan's attention focussed around his trousers. 'Are you mocking me?' she asked.

'Maybe.'

'Then maybe there isn't as much for us to discuss as I thought.'

'Don't be like that, Deirdre. It would be so nice if we could be friends.' Without invitation he rose from his chair, dragged it with an expensive-sounding screech across the polished wooden floor, and situated it within touching distance of Deirdre's left hand. A fat diamond wedding ring glinted on her finger, caught by a rogue flash of light from the busy fire.

Nathan sat. 'There, much better. There's already been too much distance between us.'

Deirdre set aside her glass of sherry. 'Are you going to tell me why you're here?'

'That's a lovely skirt, Deirdre, if not entirely practical.'

'Nathan?'

'I think you know why I'm here, but why do we have to talk business right away? Why don't we get better acquainted first.' The fire popped and crackled, reflecting in Nathan's eyes. 'Part of a successful working relationship is knowing who you're dealing with.'

'I already know all about you, Nathan.'

'Really? How interesting.'

'Your father was Irish, wasn't he?'

'With a name like O'Donnell, however did you deduce that, Miss Marple?'

'There was an incident, wasn't there?'

Nathan recoiled slightly, caught momentarily off-guard, then composed himself more carefully. 'He left my mother when I was nine years old. I can't say we ever missed him.'

'How sad.'

A twitch of anger spasmed in the corner of Nathan's mouth. He controlled it commendably. 'It was sad he chose to waste his life.'

'Died for the cause, didn't he?'

All the play had boiled away in Nathan's eyes, leaving only a simmering rage. Some small part at the back of his mind screamed at him to realise this was just an extravagant game, some childish power play Deirdre had concocted and not something he should rise to, but his words were bitterly acidic when he retaliated. 'His cause should have been looking after his family. We were somewhat more fragile than Ireland was.'

'Car bombs are messy things. They leave a lot of ruin behind.'

'Sometimes. Sometimes they just burn away a lot of things people would rather forget about.'

'Was your father one of those things?'

'My mother took me away from Ireland long before he ever blew himself up.'

Deirdre drew closer, revelling in Nathan's quiet discomfort. 'That must have been tough for you. Did you even go to his funeral?'

'No. But that was my mother's fault.' He snapped harshly, dangerously so.

The delicately pencilled curve of Deirdre's eyebrow peeked with curiosity. 'Really?'

Nathan drew a deep breath, renewing his smile. 'Perhaps we shouldn't waste our time with this idle chat, after all.'

'I couldn't agree more. Careless talk costs lives.'

'So why talk at all?' Without hesitation, Nathan touched Deirdre's hand. She looked at the hand as if carefully considering what this might mean. Her own hand did not withdraw.

'What do you want, Nathan?'

'Why does this have to be about wanting something? Why can't it be about needing something?'

'My husband may be old, but he isn't a fool.'

'He's left you here alone. Sounds like a fool to me.'

'I don't suggest you're here when he gets back.'

'And when is that likely to be?'

'Eight o'clock, maybe.'

Nathan looked thoughtfully at his watch. 'Five hours? It'll be a push, but I think we can make it.'

'You're skating on thin ice.'

He grinned with all the wickedness of the devil. 'Then I may as well dance,' he said.

*

Deirdre watched Nathan dressing, a cigarette hanging, unlit, from her bottom lip, silk sheets pulled around her shoulders. He was trying his best not to look at her. She was trying her best to look like she didn't care as much as she did.

'Do you miss him?' she asked, conversationally.

'Who?'

'Your father.'

'No.' A quick response. No hesitation, no pause to consider the truth.

'Not at all?'

Nathan buckled his belt, concentrating a little harder on the activity than one would think necessary. 'Maybe sometimes. I don't know. I guess, maybe I just miss the way he made me laugh.'

'Do you regret never getting the chance to say goodbye?'

Nathan made fists with white knuckles, his lips were pale and drawn. Thin, shadowless words formed between gritted teeth. 'I said goodbye to him once. I didn't need to say it again.'

'Is that what your mother told you?'

Nathan span suddenly, lunging towards Deirdre and grabbing her arms. 'You don't have the right. . .' He stopped, breathing ragged. She smelled of vanilla. 'You can't talk about my mother, you didn't know her. She was a good woman.'

He released his hold on her arms. She watched him cautiously, but without fear. 'This wasn't about sex, was it?' she asked.

Nathan buttoned his shirt, straightened his tie, didn't answer.

'What was it you came here for?'

He perched on the edge of the bed, tying his shoelaces. It was coming up to five o'clock and he had promised Lampar a result by six. Fifty quid was riding on it.

'Nathan?'

'Are you complaining?'

Deirdre kept herself composed, her dignity perhaps in question but by no means in tatters. 'You're a handsome man, Nathan, and famous as well. I doubt very much you did this for the sex.'

'You don't think I could be attracted to you?' He stood, checking his reflection in the mirror. Looking as good as always.

'Perhaps you are, but I don't think you would risk doing this if there wasn't something more at stake. Has my son said something?'

'Terence hasn't got the wit to say something I would concern myself with. I doubt even you could argue with that.'

'Still, he is assisting in the payment of your wages, isn't he?'

Nathan turned. 'Is he?'

'What's that supposed to mean?' She rose, threw on a night gown.

'Tiffany's Toast doesn't belong to Terence, does she?'

Deirdre crossed the room, opening a drinks cabinet and fixing herself a substantial shot of vodka. She drank it neat in one swallow. 'Of course the horse doesn't really belong to him,' she said. 'You think I could trust him with a beast like that? He'd probably lose her in a card game.'

'That's what I'd assumed.'

She poured another shot, vodka splashing over the side of the glass. 'Is that why you came here, to get one over on Terence?'

'I wouldn't rule that out as a possibility.'

The vodka glass clattered on the cabinet. Outside, it was already dark. 'Are you going to tell him this happened?'

Nathan shrugged, checking his hair in the mirror one last time. 'I guess that all depends on how you answer my next question.'

'He'll never believe you. Not without proof.'

'You may be right, but on the other hand, could your reputation stand the scrutiny? After what happened with the grounds' man your husband fired last summer?' She looked at him with watery eyes. He grinned. 'You're not the only one who's been doing their homework, Honey. I know as much about you as you know about me.'

'What do you want?' she asked.

'I don't want to blackmail you, Deirdre. I had a lot of fun today. I actually like you. . .' he paused, considering this. 'Yes, I think I like you, beneath all the pomp and makeup. Unfortunately, I don't like your son, and I don't want him hanging around the stables anymore. Not while I'm there.'

'Then ask him to leave.'

'I would, but I'm afraid Tiffany's Toast can't go with him.'

'Terence wouldn't agree to that.'

'Exactly. But Terence doesn't need to, does he? The horse is yours.'

Deirdre pressed her hands against the drinks cabinet, her eyes closed. She looked so lost. 'What is it you want me to say, Nathan?'

'I want you to let Mr Lampar take full control of Tiff's entries and declarations. We're running her short under Terence's management and we want her to win. That's all.'

'That's all?'

Nathan crossed the room and slipped his arms around Deirdre's waist. She allowed him to do this without releasing her hold on the refilled vodka glass. His lips brushed against her neck.

'Maybe not all,' he said.

Chapter Five

It was six o'clock, and the lads had already gone home, by the time Morgan Corelli, founder of Barrowdown Stables, finally dared to venture out to the stable blocks. At first, he just walked up and down the stalls, hands pressed together behind his back, listening to the snorting of the horses and the occasional bleat from the goat he had put in with Clairvoyant Knight in order to keep the brute calm. Then, when his breath became shallower and his portly frame less comfortable to heft, he sat on a hay bale and watched the stars blinking into existence on the black canvas of the night.

And there, beneath the gaze of the few half-lame animals he still trained, and the one decent horse he would surely lose within the next few weeks, he placed a hunting rifle in his mouth and pulled the trigger.

The click of the rifle's hammer snapping on an empty chamber did not disturb the horses, but it brought fresh tears to Corelli's eyes. It brought something else too. Despite his best efforts to beat himself into submission. It brought the resolve not to load the gun. At least, not today.

The barrel, cool and greasy, chattered between his teeth

'Damn it,' he whispered, throwing aside the rifle and settling instead on killing himself with the more traditional means of a cigar he had stashed in his jacket pocket. 'Giving up takes as much guts as carrying on, so what's the point?'

The cigar bobbed and jittered in the glow of his lighter, then sparked and puffed with blue smoke. It could so easily have been gun smoke.

'Would you notice?' He posed the question, not at the overhanging sky, with all its multitude of uncaring satellites, but at the horses he had dedicated his life to training.

As one might expect, they didn't answer, but considering not even

Corelli knew the true intent of the question, he didn't mind.

'Indeed.' He directed his attention to the glowing tip of his cigar - Cuban, and more expensive than he could afford - watching as it crumbled and flaked away with every thick, drawing breath he made. 'Doubt even I'd notice,' he said.

Clairvoyant Knight, a giant of a grey with an unusually knowing look in his eye and an unusual blaze down his forehead, snuffed and bucked his head. His sleek mane flapped attractively.

'I know what you're thinking,' Corelli said. 'Don't think I'm not thinking it too.' Another snort from the horse. 'He'd say no, anyway. I can't say anything to change that.'

Clairvoyant Knight - Clarence to the stable hands - showed his teeth in a maniacal grin. The goat, Isabelle, bleated with an unquestionably affirmative tone. Corelli chose to ignore them both.

The stars, twinkling in their crowded loneliness, remained, at least for the time being, completely impartial. 'And so you should,' Corelli said. 'So you bloody well should.'

'Should what, Sir?'

Corelli jumped at the unexpected and frighteningly close voice, his gaze skittering down to the rifle he had so recently been using as a toothpick. The voice was a female one, attached, without question, to Nina, the stable lass he had brought on last season. If she had seen what he had been about to do. . . If she had even glimpsed the gun, oiled barrel gleaming in the stable lights. . .

He kept his eyes down, broad shoulders hunched. 'Nina,' he said.

'Are you okay, Mr Corelli?'

She was hovering in the entrance to the stable block, hopping endearingly from one foot to the next with an awkward nervousness. She couldn't see the gun from there, it was hidden by the hay bales. At least she would be able to tell the police she hadn't suspected anything when they finally came round to scrape up Corelli's remains.

'You still here?' he asked, not meaning the question to come out anywhere near as sharp or vindictive as it did.

'So it would appear.'

'Any reason?' He kept the stoniness in his voice, determined to give away nothing of the fragility he felt. 'The others have already gone for the day, didn't you know that?'

'I was late in, I thought I'd make my time up.'

Corelli waved her away dismissively. 'Don't worry about that, girl, just run on home. Your father will be worried about you.' He sighed, trying to remember what the old him, the tough but fair him, might have said in these same circumstances. 'Try and be on time tomorrow. Buy an alarm clock.'

'I will, Sir.' She lingered in the entrance for a moment longer then, making a conscious decision, she took one faltering step closer. 'And my father isn't going to be too worried yet, he knows I'm a big girl.' Another step closer. Two more. 'You're thinking about Mr O'Donnell, aren't you?'

'You're a smart girl.' Corelli stood, concerned she may take one step too many and bring the gun into her field of vision. He made good use of his extensive bulk to ensure this didn't happen, aware even he might not be able to talk himself out of that particular situation. 'Do you know him?'

'We met last night at the dance, Sir. He's quite the charmer.'

Corelli stomped towards her, cigar jolting and bouncing between his clenched teeth. There was no humour in his eyes, no pleasant memories. He had the countenance of an old, bored dragon, waiting for some overzealous knight to happen by and make his day. 'Nothing charming about that man,' he said, through a billow of smoke. 'Not a damned thing.'

Nina, a testing smile frozen on her beautifully sculpted features, waited to see if there was going to be any further insight into the relationship between these two men. None was forthcoming.

'You want him to ride Clarence this weekend, don't you?' she said.

Corelli laughed, a bitter, acidic blast of warm air that echoed like an exploding shotgun in the stillness of the stable. 'You pick things up quick, girl, but you know he won't ride for me.'

'Have you asked him?'

'What do you think?'

The pair walked back the length of the stable blocks, then up to the house, a short uphill trek that tested the limits of Corelli's endurance more than it might once have done. At the house, beneath the glow of flickering security lights, the old trainer rested a hand on Nina's shoulder. 'Go home,' he said.

'Are you sure?'

'Yes.' He didn't look sure. He looked like he was screwing himself up from the inside, desperate to talk about the things he had not even dared to mention to his wife. 'Get home before your father comes around looking to cause trouble.'

'I think you should ring him,' she said. 'Maybe he'll say no. Maybe not. What have you got to lose?'

'I don't have much, girl, but pride comes free and that. . .' he stubbed out his cigar on the wall of the house, leaving a grubby black smear on the powdery stonework. 'That, I have plenty of. He took my horses, he never took that.'

'Is pride going to get you a winner at Aintree this weekend?'

Now Corelli managed to laugh. 'Jacobson, the boy who used to chase for us a little last year, is going to ride Clarence. He hasn't been too busy this season and can do with the exposure.'

'That isn't an answer.'

'It wasn't supposed to be.'

'So what is the answer?'

Corelli shook his head sadly. 'The truth is, Jacobson is never going to drag Clarence over the line in any better shape than fifth, and fifth isn't going to keep this stable operational. I don't need to spell it out to you what would happen if we lose that horse.'

'No, Sir.'

'Mr and Mrs Sidebottom, the owners, have been asking some serious questions about the horse's performance. If they realise the potential Clarence has we won't see him again for dust. He'll probably end up with Lampar.'

'Then you'll phone Mr O'Donnell?'

'You don't understand. He won't race for me. When he left. . .' Corelli turned away and spat as if to rid himself of some unpleasant memory. He wiped a hand across his greying moustache before continuing. 'A lot of owners saw their horses dropping back, falling out of the frame. Just coincidence, maybe one or two mistakes by inappropriate jocks, but it wasn't long before they started taking their horses across to Lampar.'

Corelli looked hard at Nina. She met his stare bravely. 'You aren't giving me a reason for not calling him,' she said.

'The loss of business hit us hard. I didn't think we were going to ride the storm.' He stopped, gauging Nina's expression. 'We all do things we regret, girl. He'll never forgive me for my mistakes.'

'And you won't even give him the chance?'

'The last time we met he wouldn't even look at me, let alone speak. I hurt him as badly as I ever thought he hurt me. It's been too long since then.'

The night crowded in, straining to hear the unspoken thoughts jostling between the trainer and the stable lass. The unnatural chitter of bats in the darkness was the only other sound. 'What happened between you two?' Nina asked. As she spoke, thunder rumbled heavily in the distance, proclaiming the arrival of a long-expected storm. The stars flickered off one by one as strings of invisible black clouds, like deadly assassins, stretched across the sky.

Corelli fumbled a ring of keys from his pocket and opened the front door of a house he had given up on trying to pay for. The receivers would be visiting within the next few weeks. After that, who knew what he would be able to do to keep himself from loading that rifle. 'Go home,' he repeated, thought for a moment, then added: 'Or join me for a drink.'

Nina touched his arm gently. She could almost feel the sadness radiating off him. 'I'll go,' she said. 'But promise me you'll think about this some more. Mr Lampar isn't planning on putting anything out at Aintree. Nathan might be available.'

Corelli pushed the door open. 'I promise I'll think about this some more,' he said, and the first drops of rain began to fall.

*

The fire, in its blackened, stone hearth, crackled and spat, coughing smoke into the flue. Corelli watched the flames intently, occasionally feeding them another bundle of paper that would hiss and splutter before disintegrating into a flurry of black snow.

'Do you want to tell me what this is all about?' his wife, Charlotte, asked. He chose to ignore the question completely.

In the twisting, light-dark patterns of the fire, Corelli's eyes shone like opals set in deep wells. Behind those eyes the arguments blazed as hot as any inferno. His smile was a hybrid grimace.

'Morgan?' Charlotte curled her feet up underneath her on the couch. It had been week's since they had spoken to one another other than to say 'good morning' or 'good night'. Morgan was sliding, she knew that, sliding into some other place, some world where she couldn't reach him anymore. Something was wrong and she couldn't find a way in to put things right.

Another bundle of papers, papers Charlotte had never been privy to before, exploded in a shower of sparks, momentarily shivering the shadows of the room into contorted, laughing faces. Morgan Corelli, small-time trainer and part-time husband, continued staring into the hearth. In the other place, the place where Charlotte couldn't go, and perhaps didn't really want to go; in the place where Morgan battled every day for a reason not to load his hunting rifle, a phone was ringing.

- Hello.
- Who is this?
- It's been a long time, Nathan, but surely not long enough to forget me.

- Mr Corelli. What an unexpected surprise.

- Not an entirely unpleasant one, I hope.

- You've got a lot of nerve ringing me here. Have you been drinking?

- I'm dry now. You know that.

- There are so many things I thought I knew about you, Mr Corelli. I thought you were a decent man. I also thought you had some pride.

- Pride is somewhat overrated. I'm sure you're aware of that, Nathan.

- How's your wife?

- Fine.

- I hear they let her out of the hospital.

- That's right.

- I'm surprised she came back. Is she that desperate to sink with you?

- How did you ever get so mean, boy? I never brought you up to -

- You never brought me up. You understand? You were never my father.

- Of course not. That's not what I meant. I just meant you never used to be this way. What happened to that bright-eyed kid we all loved?

- He woke up.

Corelli blinked away the memory of that hurtful conversation, a rogue tear blurring his vision momentarily. There were three more bundles of paper left. Three more neatly tied collections of hand-written notes. Damn those notes. Damn everything they stood for, everything they cost him.

He glanced over his shoulder. Charlotte was watching him, but there was nothing in her eyes, they were as milky and lifeless as the night he had almost lost her. That night after the incident.

He tried a nervous smile. She smiled back. Soon she was going to need to know the truth about the rest of this sorry charade. The part where he lost everything.

Another package of letters hit the flames in a puff of ash and sparkles. The fire roared hungrily, digesting the hurt he had never been able to recover from. In his head, the voices. . .

- I need your help, Nathan.

- Why am I not surprised?

- Barrowdown Stables is in trouble. I'm in trouble. We're losing horses, too many horses. Nobody wants to ride them and I can't find a winning opportunity, not even for the best.

- And this is my problem because. . ?

- It isn't your problem, Nathan. I just thought. . . I don't know. Maybe what we used to have, the way things were. Maybe that meant something.

- Perhaps you should have thought about that before.

- You were like my family.

- You were never like mine. What you did to us, what you thought you could do to us. . . I can't forgive you for that.

- I'm not asking you to forgive me, Nathan. I'm asking you to ride for me. I've got a horse here, better than I deserve. He's a beauty, you'd love him. Plenty of strength, leads from the off. You'd be perfect for him, just what he needs for a win.

- Just what you need to stay in business.

- I won't deny that. I need your help more than you need mine, but another win isn't going to hurt your career any, is it?

- True enough, but I have more than enough work on for Lampar. I don't need to take on your troubles as well.

- It's one race.

- Then another, and another.

- One race.

Charlotte stood, a stilted motion, like that of a marionette in the hands of an amateur. 'I'm going to bed,' she said.

'Good night,' Morgan said, without looking back.

There were two lots of letters left. Once they were gone, there would be nothing remaining of his affair. Maybe then this would end.

Maybe then he could atone for the things he had done.

'Why did you bother?' Charlotte asked, her voice full of contempt.

Morgan pulled free a single letter, unfolded it. The handwriting was small and neat, perfectly legible even after all this time. 'I don't know,' he said. 'I thought we could make it work.'

'You should have left me,' she said.

'I know.'

- I know you've got plenty on for Lampar, but this horse runs over three miles. He's running at Aintree this weekend. You haven't got anything on at Aintree, I know you haven't.

- Actually, not necessarily true. We do have a horse lined up for that race.

- But. . .

- I had to sweet talk the owners, but Tiffany's Toast is going to get to stretch her legs after all. I'm sorry, I won't be able to race for you.

- Tiffany runs short of three miles. She always has done.

- Times are changing, Mr Corelli.

- Nathan, please?

- Change with them, Mr Corelli.

'You bastard,' Corelli whispered, screwing up the letter and feeding it to the fire. 'It was one race. I only wanted one race.'

Charlotte, still standing in the doorway, watched quietly.

'You were my last chance,' he said. 'I know I've done some bad things, but you were all I had left. You were my family.'

Charlotte wiped the tears out of her eyes and closed the door.

Corelli picked up the last bundle of letters. These were the ones he had shown to Nathan.

He threw them on the fire, swallowed hard.

Everything was gone.

It was a year ago today that his wife had woken up in a hospital bed and looked him in the eyes. There, bathed in the white-yellow heat of overhead lights, drowning in the stench of disinfectant, tubes and needles stuck in her face and arms, she had beckoned him closer.

In a cracked and ruined voice, like the articulation of his shattered life, she had spoken to him.

'I didn't want you to save me,' she had said.

Chapter Six

Aintree...

The bustle, the noise. Outrageous hats, a generous sun tearing yellow strips through thinning clouds. The snuff and bellow of excited horses, the incessant drone of the bookies. Smart suits, brandy glasses, panicked trainers on mobile phones. Ambulances, coffee, stable hands hurrying to throw saddle cloths over skittish fillies. The smell of freshly torn clods of turf, tinny voices over loud-speakers, cameras, television pundits with microphones. Smiling jocks, a constant, teeming crowd of eager staff milling about. Land Rovers, Guiness, voices raised in laughter, the clap of hands on backs. Money. The crisp smell of folding money.

So much money.

Then, through the crowd, into the weighing room where the exuberant mood is replaced with quiet anticipation, the hushed conversation of old colleagues discussing tactics for the race ahead. In here, where silks hang on dedicated pegs, yellow and pink and silver, there are no expectant crowds, no microphones, no autographs. Here, there is only the jockeys.

'Neil Jacobson, it's been a while.'

'Nathan, you old dog.' Neil Jacobson dropped his kit on the bench and extended a hand. Nathan accepted the hand gratefully. 'It's been too long. So good to see you again.'

'I hear you got yourself an animal to be reckoned with, Neil.'

'That's what the old timer tells me. I hope you're prepared to eat a little mud.'

'After the cooking Lampar's staff have been dishing up, I'm looking forward to it.'

They laughed together, in the slightly uncomfortable way that old friends, who are not so close as once they might have been, laugh. The laughter tailed off suddenly and there was a deafening silence only idle chatter about nothing could fill.

'How's life been treating you?' Nathan stepped back, examining Neil thoughtfully. 'Perhaps a little too well, judging by the timber round the middle.'

'It's not as easy as it used to be. Not since I gave up the smokes.'

'You quit smoking?'

'Apparently they're bad for your health. Speaking of which, I hear you were sniffing around Barrowdown the other day, looking for new acquisitions.'

Nathan raised a humoured eyebrow. 'By which you mean?'

'The stable girl, Nina. Rumour has it you took her out. . . riding.'

Nathan looked away, busying himself with changing into the green and red silks of the Cavanaugh family. The jockeys would be called through to the scales any time now. 'I didn't know she worked for Corelli,' he said, trying to keep the tone airy.

'Small world.'

'Too small.' He laughed quietly, distractedly.

'And you're sure you didn't know she worked for Corelli?'

'Not until the morning after.'

'Hangover?'

'The worst.' Nathan was aware of several pairs of eyes watching him. Suddenly the weighing room seemed too small for all the people in it. 'I swear. There's no way I would have taken her. . . riding, if I'd known she was one of Corelli's.' He thought about this, wondered if it was even remotely true.

'That's what I thought.' Neil leaned closer. 'I never thought for a second you might have done it in order to find out how the Governor was doing these days.' His eyes were knowing. 'That's just something some of the lads were saying this morning. Still. . .' He straightened up. 'All in the past now, I take it. You never were one to plough the field twice.'

Nathan's grin widened. 'So how many people has she told?' Perhaps there was a little too much eagerness in his voice. Perhaps

. . . hope.'

'She's got a big mouth, that one. I think it may have got her in a little trouble.'

'Trouble?'

'Turned up with a black eye yesterday. They say her father has a matching one for you.'

For a moment Nathan pictured Nina's face, black makeup traded in for an unsightly bruise. He forced the image away aggressively. 'How does this sort of thing always happen to me?'

'So many adoring fans, Nathan.'

'How big is her father?'

'Huge.'

They finished changing in silence. Around them the other jockeys continued to discuss riding plans. Nathan tried to listen in on all the different conversations at once. Tried to do anything but think about the girl with the panda eyes.

' - can't keep it up over three miles - '

' - just in behind the leader. The mud can seriously fly when this - '

' - runner of Corelli's gets in gear - '

' - but if we can hold it together we may well be able to get a head up at the last - '

' - if the jumping's good.'

Nathan smiled to himself, giving away nothing behind a poker face of chiselled ice. Nobody asked what his intentions were, they already knew. He intended to win, and he intended to win with style, from the front. There were a few strong contenders in the field and the good-to-soft going would be a real test. Even so, he was quietly confidant - no, he was deadly certain - Tiffany's Toast had more than enough muscle to make the running.

'Nathan.'

Nathan looked back at Neil. 'What?'

'Don't think I don't know I'm the second choice for this ride.'

'Second choice?'

'The Governor rang you, didn't he?'
'Does it matter?'
'No.'
'So why ask?'
'Did you consider going back for him?'
'Maybe.'
'You know they aren't running for him anymore. It's all slipping away from him. I don't think I can change that.'
'You're a good jock, Neil. Just go out there and prove what you can do.' Nathan's smile broadened to the point of severing the top of his head. 'And besides, second place isn't so bad.'
'This horse, this Clairvoyant Knight. It isn't going to touch you, is it?'
Nathan shook his head. 'Sorry, mate, it hasn't got a chance.'

*

In the scales, the chamber off from the weighing room, where the actual weighing took place, Glen Lampar was waiting to personally receive Nathan's saddle. Lampar's smile said everything that needed to be said about his belief in Tiffany's Toast's ability to take a first spot in this sort of company.

'I hope you haven't forgotten,' Nathan said, passing Lampar the saddle.

'Forgotten what?'
'You owe me for getting the horse out over this distance.'
'Oh yes, that little wager we had.'
'Fifty quid, you said.'
'If you pull this horse over the line in first you'll see a little more than fifty quid.'

'The bet was on getting the horse here today, not winning with it. Lady Cavanaugh can be a tough woman when she wants to be. I had to do some serious sweet-talking to organise this.'

'More than sweet-talking, I'd wager.'
'Sometimes it's hard to be me.'

Lampar laughed, the hearty deep sound of a man about to make himself a lot of money. He had been seriously backing Nathan all morning and Tiffany's Toast was certainly looking good for the payout, despite this being her first outing over three miles. 'I just hope whatever you did to get her here was worth it,' he said.

Nathan winked, a twinkling memory in his eye. 'Believe me, Governor, it was worth it.'

*

'Jockeys.' The magic word.

Tiffany's Toast bucked agitatedly, eyes wide and damp, ears sweating. Her brown flanks heaved and bulged, glistening wet, heart thudding alarmingly. Nathan patted her shoulders, willing her calm.

The flag raised, snapping like a thirsty tongue in the wind.

Nathan drew breath, squeezing his eyes shut, letting the world drop away.

There was the distant, barely perceived stamp of hooves, muted sounds from the excited crowd. A snort, accompanied by white fume, escaped from Tiff's flared nostrils.

Twelve runners, a garish collection of blue and silver and red silk, squashed together in a jostling pack of rippling muscle. The horses whinnied and pawed at the earth, the jocks adjusted their grips, lengthening or shortening the reigns. The seconds ticked by. Ticked, so slowly.

The Earth ground to a halt.

Then there was only the blasting resonance of Nathan's own heartbeat, tattooing barely perceived fear against the inside of his ribcage. He had been there a hundred times before, silks glistening and slick in the glow of the persistently obtrusive sunshine. But this time was different. Somehow, in a way he could not explain, this was different.

He was situated outside of the pack; here there would be less excitement for the unblinkered Tiff' to be concerned with. She would have the space she needed to make early ground.

Nathan glanced across at Jacobson, three from the inside. He would need to use a little muscle to clear through, but his horse was virtually chewing its way through the tape with anticipation. Strength wasn't an issue here.

This was all new to Tiff', an unexpected slog after six months of half-hearted flirtations with serious competition. She was really going to have to prove herself now.

A breathless pause.

The magic word. The God voice.

Jockeys.

Now.

The flag dropped, the horses lurched into stride, hooves chomping deep rivets in the turf. The wind roared into fresh vigour, tearing at pink-blue silk, swirling the viper's hiss of rain into spiralling, stinging eddies. Nathan, whip straight and guiding, dipped low in the saddle. He could feel Tiff's heart thudding beneath him, a machine as powerful as any car, demanding respect.

Clumps of earth shuddering out behind him, Nathan skilfully guided Tiff' to the head of the crowd. As suspected, the space had proven useful, getting Tiff' into shape for the next two miles before the real race with the strongest opposition began.

The horses started to bunch, dropping into preordained positions.

To his left, one of the riders, not Jacobson, veered dangerously. Without thinking, without given the time to think, Nathan edged across, using Tiff's muscle to force a space out in front. The thunder of hooves was a drowning wave, arcing up behind him like a tsunami. He remained still in the saddle, using only his heels and the quivering line of his whip to keep Tiff' straight. From a distance, he would barely have looked like he was trying.

For a moment, two moments, Nathan was entirely alone, then there was a flash of pink silk coming up fast. Jacobson was pushing alongside him, a manic, excited grin on his muddied face.

The first hurdle was approaching.

Nathan remained calm, dipped in the saddle, and let Tiff' do the jumping. There was a dull clump, the jump bending beneath the horse's weight. Not a good clearance. Tiff' landed out of stride and staggered uncomfortably. Jacobson moved inside, a pink blur on the green canvas of the track.

Nathan, determined not to let Tiff' drop back and lose confidence, repositioned himself, straightened his whip and pressed his heels against her flanks. For a moment she wobbled, then she was in full stride again, closing down on Jacobson.

Mud flew, grass clods smacking against Nathan's goggles as he dipped in behind Clairvoyant Knight and then pulled level.

There were other horses nearby, fuming and snorting and bellowing, huge limbs driven like hydraulic pistons into the chewed earth, but Nathan remained focussed, looking only to gain those vital inches against Jacobson. A nose ahead and Tiff' was unbeatable.

The second hurdle loomed up suddenly. Out of step, Tiff' was taken by surprise. Nathan rose up in the saddle, rearranging the horse's legs. The jump was taken late, costing ground, but it was clean. The landing was perfect. Behind him there was the familiar, sickening clatter of a horse that hadn't made the jump. There was the dull thud of a jockey hitting the earth.

Nathan got low again, picking up the pace. Jump after jump. Better.

This was better.

At the next hurdle Tiff' got her nose up on Clairvoyant Knight and she was away, an unstoppable dark wind blazing across the track. Her head dipped and bobbed rhythmically, hypnotically. Behind, still in a position to challenge Tiff' over the next mile, a crowd of three younger horses pounded and stamped, breath pluming, flanks steaming, jockeys hunkered like psychedelic monkeys in the saddle. But always it was Jacobson and Clarence that forced Tiff's pace, keeping tight to her left flank, threatening to edge through. Nathan knew what Jacobson was trying to do, trying to make Tiff' blow up with six furlongs left to travel, but Tiff' had too much in reserve, more than any of these other jocks could imagine.

Nathan's grin widened, the wind cut into him like a knife. He was alive.

Another jump, and Nathan didn't even need to force the issue. Tiff' took off without thinking and lengthened her stride on the landing. Jacobson, pink smudge on grey, dropped back by a half length. Nathan took the chance to coax Tiff' harder. Another half length and Jacobson, his confidence already low, would drop out of the running entirely. This was as much about mind games as it was about making the jumps.

Clarence was strong though, with stamina in buckets, and Jacobson's less than gentle handling of the old brute seemed to be working. He was already closing the gap. Clarence's nostrils were flaring and wet, his muscular chest shuddering with each hammering stride.

Nearing the two mile mark, the two horses were shoulder to shoulder, Jacobson forcing inside against the white railing of the track, desperate for any extra space he could put between himself and Nathan.

The rest of the pack began to falter, slipping out of contention, unable to knock up a gear and threaten the two forerunners as they galloped towards the second to last hurdle. Two lengths, three lengths, the leaders pushed ahead, racing only each other, barely aware of another fall behind them, the bitter cry of a horse rolling, a jockey tucking himself into ball as he bounced off the turf, awful, searing pain ripping through ligaments in his knee.

Nathan risked a glance over his left shoulder. Jacobson was sat on his knee, his whip poised, ready to blur into motion as soon as they touched down from the next hazard.

Even then, the wind squealing around them in a hideous orchestration, the two jocks managed to grin at each other. The horses spared each other no such courtesy.

The jump.

Tiff' was in the air a fraction of a second before Clarence and perhaps that distracted Jacobson, caused a momentary lapse of concentration. Whatever the reason, when Tiff' slammed into the earth on the far side of the jump, the bone-jolting shock shivering through her front legs, Jacobson was already spilling out of the saddle. Nathan was vaguely aware of the crunch of a human body pounding into the turf, of Clarence's huge, grey mass dropping close behind him. Then nothing. Nobody.

Nathan, whip at shoulder height, shaking with anticipation for what should have been a desperate struggle over the distance to the last hurdle, looked back. Clarence was cantering along the railing, bucking his head and bellowing with an inarticulate fury. A pink mess of silk and awkwardly positioned limbs was crumpled in the middle of the track. Other horses, runners Nathan had hardly been aware of for the last mile of the race, were skirting round the shattered remains of Jacobson, too far behind to be of any risk to Tiff's first spot.

Nathan faced front, took the last jump at barely more than a canter and eased into the final straight. There was no smile on his face as he crossed the line.

*

After the pounding drumbeat of the horses' hooves, there was silence, then, as if the patiently waiting world was crashing back into place, noise. The familiar, snapping, flashing, shouting, cheering, smiling, over-enthusiastic noise.

Nathan headed towards the winners' enclosure, already dropping down from the saddle. He braced himself as the swarm of usual bodies pressed around. Owners, trainers, reporters. Women.

Cameras exploded excitedly, freezing the world in great, white gulps. Nathan forced his best smile and waved at the crowd. Microphones were waving under his nose, television crews unspooling metres of cable as they ran cameras into place. Tiff' chomped on her bit, stamping the earth as a stable lass took the reigns from Nathan. Smiling. Everyone was smiling.

'How's Neil?' Nathan asked the closest microphone.

'How do you feel?' the microphone - some Sunday newspaper - asked back.

'Is Neil hurt?'

There was a hand on his shoulder. 'Dear boy,' the owner of the hand, Glen Lampar, was saying. 'Dear boy, that was most thrilling. Most thrilling.' He was talking at Nathan but his eyes were tracking the position of the nearest reporters that were likely to put his face on the front page of their newspaper.

Microphones everywhere.

'What happened to Neil?' Nathan asked.

'Mr O'Donnell. This was Tiffany's Toast's first outing over this kind of distance. We understand it was partly your suggestion to give it a try.'

Nathan gazed dumbly at the young female reporter talking at him while she simultaneously attempted to keep the camera rolling on her good side. 'Something like that,' he said. 'Mr Lampar thought it would be worth a try and I was prepared to take the risk.' Nathan was coasting, running out the age-old stuff he gave to all these people. They didn't care whose idea it was, they would decide that for themselves. All these people wanted was a memorable quote for the headline.

'It looks like Glen was right. So where does Tiff" go from here? Surely you'll be looking to get her some black type in a listed race.'

'Is there any word on Neil?' Nathan persisted. 'I saw him go down on the second-last.'

'Initial report says he's fine. Just bruising. Do you think he might have taken the win if things had gone differently?'

Camera flash. Say cheese. Blink the world back into focus. Still smiling.

'I don't like to talk about 'mights'. Neil was pushing me hard towards the end and I think he might have had a good chance of lasting if he could have kept it together. I was sorry to see him drop.'

There was some jostling in the crowd, a furious Corelli pushing unwary onlookers out of his way in a flurry of activity that belied his usually unobtrusive demeanour. 'You,' he said, pointing, aware of the flashing cameras that would immortalise his outrage. 'You were crowding in on Clarence through the whole race. Bad form, I say. Bloody bad form.'

Nathan grinned. 'I'm glad to hear Neil's not hurt. I'm sorry he couldn't get you a place. You've got yourself a good horse there, he nearly had me.' Nathan, even through the crowd, could see the mill of disgruntled racegoers standing around Clarence, tutting and frowning as the stable lass threw a cloth over the beast's broad, misting flanks. 'Next time he might get me.'

'There is no next time,' Corelli spat. 'No bloody next time. No bloody horse.'

Nathan frowned, puzzled, but before he could query Corelli's remarks he was being ushered towards a large camera on a tripod where a middle-aged chap wearing earphones was signalling 'on three' to an impossibly attractive reporter in an impossibly short skirt. Nathan allowed himself to be ushered without argument. He could see Lampar at the other end of the paddock motioning to him to 'go and get bloody weighed'. He indicated that he understood and then turned on his most handsome smile. The camera focussed in on him like a huge, unblinking eye. And on two, on one. . .

'You're on.'

Nathan. How do you feel? It must be so exciting. You're thrilled obviously. You really deserve it. Must be proud. Glen must be overjoyed. You probably can't wait to get it finalised. Won't keep you any more. Just a final word to the viewers. How do you feel?

How do you feel?

Everybody wants to know. How do you feel?

As Nathan attempted to explain what a great thrill it was to take a first over this kind of distance with a horse that might well have balked at the challenge, he couldn't help but be aware that in the crowd, not far from where Corelli had fumed and fussed, a large man in a perfectly pressed black suit watched him, in much the same way as many other people were watching him, with a hand-rolled cigarette pressed between the thin line of his lips and the beginnings of a smile that could have so easily been a sneer etched into his stern features.

Just another admiring fan. But the memory of that one onlooker lingered with Nathan for the rest of the day and later, even after what was about to happen with Corelli, it was that memory that woke him rudely from troubled dreams.

Chapter Seven

During the celebrations - 'Drinks' as Lampar liked to call them - the moods were varied to say the least. Lady Cavanaugh, looking as splendid as always in a low cut, backless dress of ruffled black silk, was as much a vision of excitement as she was an exciting vision. Her husband, the diminutive Lord, quaffed his champagne eagerly enough, but there was a look in his eyes that betrayed his general disinterest in the whole situation. Terence Cavanaugh sat in the corner, picking at the dainties Lampar's housemaids had laid on at short notice, talking to himself and occasionally firing a razorblade glare at Nathan. The stable hands were pleased enough, and Lampar was as drunk on euphoria as he was on his own free-flowing alcohol.

Nathan acknowledged every time someone congratulated him, but he was too distracted to extract any enjoyment from the perpetual back-slapping and inane comments. He was thinking about Corelli, about his comments at the racetrack.

'No bloody next time. No bloody horse.'

Twice he had picked up the phone to call the trainer. Twice he had told himself not to get involved.

'Nathan. Nathan. Sweetheart. You are an absolute delight.'

Nathan screwed up the thick slab of disquiet that had settled in his gut and allowed a smile to blaze across his troubled features once more as the beautiful Lady Cavanaugh floated towards him. She managed to put as much wiggle in her walk as was humanly possible. She appeared to have already forgotten that it was largely due to blackmail that she was in this situation at all.

'I'm glad I could finally get that win for you,' Nathan said, with only the slightest hint of triumph in his voice.

She embraced him tightly, allowing her hands to run down his back a little further than he actually felt comfortable with. Her lips pressed against his ear in what, to any onlooker, would have looked like a friendly kiss. 'Meet me upstairs,' she whispered.

Nathan glanced across at Deirdre's husband, who was poking around at some caviar with a cracker and wrinkling his nose with champagne bubbles. He had never been interested in the horses, probably wasn't interested in his wife, and was clearly only here for the spread. If Deirdre vanished he would barely even notice, at least, not until he looked for someone to warm him up in the back of the Limousine on the way home.

'Follow me in two minutes,' Lady Cavanaugh said.

Nathan said, a little louder than was necessary, 'Here's to the next win.' He watched her walk away, transfixed gaze following every bounce, every beautifully, carefully planned step.

One of Lampar's maids dashed by holding a tray of bubblingly full champagne glasses. Nathan stopped her and took a glass, downing the contents in one shot. He checked his watch, took another glass. 'Thanks,' he said, indicating the maid could move on. He drank the champagne as slowly as he was able.

It was amazing how long two minutes could be.

Once the two minutes were up, he waited a further thirty seconds, which was about as fashionably late as he could bear to be after having already seen the dress Deirdre was wearing.

He took the stairs two at a time.

The room she had selected was one of the disused masters in the west wing. The housemaids only ran a duster around these rooms every once in a while and most of the furniture was shapeless humps under large, white sheets. The windows had curtains up and shutters pulled across on the outside. When the door was shut on the light from the hallway, it was almost black inside.

'Deirdre?' Nathan said, pressing his back to the door. His voice seemed harsh and loud and worse, desperate, in the silence. The smell of dust - stale, lifeless things - was in the air.

A shape, a body, moved in the darkness and for a moment - one crazy moment - Nathan had visions of a tall man in a pressed suit lunging at him through the gloom. Then soft hands were touching his face, warm lips pressing against his. His arms wrapped around the body. Somewhere along the way the ruffled silk had been discarded and his hands ran over smooth skin.

'I didn't know if you'd follow,' the body said, lying smoothly.

'I had a spare five minutes,' Nathan said, hearing, rather than feeling, his belt buckle being undone.

'You were magnificent today.'

'Babe, I'm just getting started.'

The body pressed against his, the sounds of the party downstairs rose up, muffled and distant. Cheering. Lampar's voice calling for silence. Christ, don't ask for a speech. Don't ask for. . . A hand slid up under Nathan's shirt and then he was past caring, guessing at the location of the bed and throwing the body towards it. Dustsheets billowed around them, old mattress springs creaked.

'My husband suspects something's going on,' the body said, as elegant fingers worked around Nathan's shirt buttons. In his pocket, something was vibrating. Damned mobile phone.

'How do you know?' he asked.

'It's in his eyes. After you left the other night, when he came home, he looked at me. He just looked and it was like he knew.'

'Has he actually said anything?'

'No.'

'Then forget about it. It's nothing.' He allowed the body to envelope him totally. 'It's nothing.'

Nothing.

The phone in his pocket stopped vibrating.

Nothing.

*

Before returning downstairs, which he did without even sparing time for the traditional cigarette, Nathan made certain his clothing was arranged as it had been prior to his encounter with Lady Cavanaugh. He left her lounging on the bed, surrounded by damp, white sheets.

She seemed happy enough to be left.

The party was already winding down by that stage and most of the stable hands, never for one moment forgetting the six o'clock start they all faced, had dispersed in a flurry of smiles and waves and 'Well dones' and 'Top forms'. Terence had also left, probably with an inarticulate 'humph' or similar well-educated remark. Lord Cavanaugh had resorted to dozing in one of the easy chairs, a half-glass of champagne trembling precariously in one liver-spotted hand.

Lampar met Nathan on the stairs. 'Party not to your style?' he asked. His words had soaked up a great deal of alcohol and had become artificially inflated in volume. The acid level was up too.

'Not much in the way of talent,' Nathan said. 'My reputation is a little too much for most of your stable lasses to deal with.'

'Your reputation is a little too much for pretty much everyone. You'll be forced to leave the county before too long.'

'If not the country.'

The same old banter as always; humour, disguising a more serious undercurrent.

'I've told you before, just be careful. The last thing this stable needs is your stupid mug splashed all over the tabloids because some little stable girl says you couldn't keep it in your trousers.'

Nathan slapped Lampar on the shoulder. 'You worry too much.'

'You don't worry enough.'

'Governor, I have a lot of love to share. I can't deny what I am.'

Lampar's grin furrowed the wrinkles around his mouth and eyes, but through those beaming teeth it was possible to see the handsome young man he once had been. A young man that had, perhaps, done many of the things Nathan now did. 'I don't even know what you are,' Lampar said. 'But I don't want you turning my stables into the laughing stock of the racing community.'

'Everybody loves a comedian, Boss.'

'But nobody loves a clown. Now get out of here. You got an early start tomorrow.'

'Best ring me,' Nathan said, remembering the missed phone call to his mobile.

'You want me to bring you coffee too?'

'Black. No sugar.'

'Anything else?'

'I'll let you know.'

Nathan bounded past Lampar and headed for the front door. As he passed through the reception, where the last of the party guests were sorting out jackets and fur coats and umbrellas, he pulled the phone out of his pocket. One missed call. One answer phone message.

He didn't recognise the number. He thought of perfect suits and sunglasses.

He swallowed hard.

The room continued to move around him, guests evaporating into the dark of the night. People were tapping him on the shoulder. Thank you. Well done. Thank you. Good job.

He rang the answer phone service.

'Nathan. . . Mr O'Donnell. Mr Big Shot. You make me sick, you bloody coward. You make me sick. You make me. . . damn it. Shit. It's all gone. You hear me? The stable, the horse, the bloody, bloody . . . the bloody lot. It's all gone, you little shit.'

Mr Corelli, his biggest fan. Drunk, unsurprisingly.

Nathan checked his watch. Eleven-thirty.

He deleted the message, slipped the phone back into his trouser pocket. Corelli had sounded in a bad way, worse than just drunk.

He walked back to his cottage at the edge of the stable grounds.

Corelli had wanted to speak to him for some reason. He had wanted to speak to him at Aintree, but interviews had got in the way. He had wanted to tell Nathan something important. The question was, did Nathan want to hear?

He looked at his front door key. Looked at the keys to his Jag'.

Did he want to hear?

He unlocked the car and pulled out of the stables, gravel crunching and spitting under the tyres.

Perhaps he was making a big mistake, but even through the anger it was obvious to see that the phone call had not been intended to be a stream of abuse. It had been a request for assistance.

Nathan had never been much in the way of helping anyone other than himself, but Corelli, despite everything, had helped him once.

The Jag' squealed out onto the deserted road, the lights knocked up to full-beam to pick a route through the twisting back routes leading to Corelli's stables. Nathan drove carefully, playing a new CD on the stereo and singing along to the choruses he knew and humming along to the verses he didn't, but all the time there was a nagging thought at the back of his mind. The nagging thought told him to turn the car right around and go home, go to bed, leave Corelli to sober up.

He ignored the thought and kept driving.

When he arrived at Barrowdown Stables, the gates were standing open, almost as though his arrival was expected, and he was able to drive up to the front door of the house without rousing anyone.

The house was unlit. Not a single light shimmering from between cracks in the heavy curtains. An unsettling quiet lay upon the surroundings, almost as if the night itself had smothered the stables to death.

But it was late. Everybody was asleep. Of course everybody was asleep. What had he expected? A welcoming committee?

He pulled the mobile phone out of his pocket and looked at it, considered phoning somebody. Anybody. Hi, just in the neighbourhood. Would you mind. . ?

No.

Ridiculous idea.

He slipped the phone into his jacket.

The blackness of the dead house appeared to stretch up into the sky, expanding to engulf the world. What if Corelli had done something?

Turn around.

Deal with this tomorrow.

Drive away.

He got out of the car.

Damn, it was cold. He buttoned his jacket, wishing he had thought to bring an overcoat.

He shoved his hands deep into his trouser pockets and made for the front door of the house, uncertain of what he was intending to do when he got there. Knock? Wake up the whole house to ask if Mr Corelli, a man he despised, was okay?

Must be crazy. Should have just forgotten all about it, gone to bed. Maybe he should have phoned one of the girls in his little black book to keep him company, make him feel better in that way only naked female bodies were able to. Corelli was not, and never had been, his concern.

He passed under the security light, wondered briefly why it didn't flash on and trap him in its dazzling white beam.

Then something. . .

It hit him hard in the side of the face and knocked him flat against the wall of the house. The mobile phone flew out of his jacket and skittered away with a broken twang.

For a terrible moment there was that looming shadow again, the perfect, black suit, then Nathan spiralled off the edge of the universe into the equally perfect blackness of unconsciousness.

Chapter Eight

Eventually the world swam back into focus and with it came a green wave of nausea. Also with it came Corelli and what, from first impressions, appeared to be a hunting rifle, the muzzle of which was, unnervingly enough, pointing in Nathan's general direction and bobbing drunkenly. The bobbing was possibly the worst thing.

'So nice of you to join me,' Corelli spat, and the words sounded like whiskey poured over ice. 'You must be missing your party.'

Nathan shook his head, trying to shuffle recent events into a coherent order. The drive, the moment of indecision in the car, the. . . The security light. Corelli had taken out the security light. He had planned it. He had planned this whole thing. Cold fear choked Nathan's lungs like splinters. 'Always a pleasure to reschedule my social calendar for an old friend,' he said. The words were thick in his throat.

'You're late.'

Nathan blinked and was horrified when blood dripped from his eyelid. How badly injured was he?

He forced his head up, forced himself to look around. Pay attention. Details were important. Details could save his life.

He was in the colt quadrangle of the stables, sat with his back to a stack of hay bales. Corelli was sat opposite, an empty whiskey bottle in his right hand, the rifle held awkwardly in his left hand. Corelli's trembling finger was resting, not-so-casually, on the rifle's trigger.

Nathan tried to concentrate. How had he got into this situation?

Corelli had taken out the security light. That's how. This wasn't a spur of the moment thing. Corelli had organised it.

'Late?' Nathan groaned, arranging himself more comfortably. 'Looks like I wasn't late enough. Any chance of a coffee?'

'You should have been here to ride Clairvoyant Knight. You were meant to ride him.' There was a snort of agreement from one of the stable blocks, few of which, Nathan noticed, were still in use. 'The owners think I'm incompetent, they're taking him away. Without that horse I'm lost.'

'You'll get by,' Nathan said. His head throbbed angrily.

'Not this time. The stables are being sold off to clear my debts. I should imagine Clarence will end up with you and Lampar, most of my staff too.'

'And this is your answer? To wave a gun around in my face? What happened to you, Corelli? What in the name of God made you this way?'

Corelli was silent.

'Was it me? Is this all about me?'

'Hasn't it always been about you? That's the way you like it, isn't it? Always got to be the centre of the universe and all else be damned.' Corelli blasted a short and uncommonly callous laugh between his teeth. 'Give a beggar a horse and he'll ride to the devil.'

'What's that supposed to mean?'

'I gave you everything you ever had. I put you where you are today.'

'I put myself here.'

Corelli threw the empty whiskey bottle over his shoulder and took a firmer grip on the rifle. The bottle shattered in the darkness. 'All I asked was one ride. One ride for everything I did for you.'

'Everything you did?' Anger blazed up inside Nathan, blanketing the fear and nausea. 'You killed my father, you bastard.'

Corelli shook his head sadly. 'You still believe that, don't you? Even after all this time. Your father killed himself. He died for his beliefs, not for anything I may have done to him.'

'That you did do to him.'

'He was going back to Ireland anyway, your mother couldn't stop him. I didn't split them up, they split themselves up, and I sure as hell didn't put that bomb in his hand.'

'You may as well have done. He couldn't function without my mother. He loved her.'

Corelli rose and somehow, somehow, he appeared huge. The gun waved and zagged, his finger itching over the trigger. 'Yes,' he spat. 'He loved her. She'd show up for work every day with his love, his bloody possessive love, showing all over her face. A fresh bruise for every time he needed to prove how much he cared.'

'He had every right to be possessive.'

'I wasn't even seeing your mother. I wanted to.' He laughed, choked back exasperated, sad tears. 'She wouldn't even look at me. She loved him as hard as ever he hit her and there was no room for me between them. It was your father that pushed her away, pushed her towards me. He was to blame.'

'You're a damned liar, Corelli.'

'I never expected you to believe that I didn't become involved with your mother until after your father died, but that's the truth. He pushed her and pushed her and one day she pushed back. While you were down at the stables. . .' he gestured at his surroundings with a defeated wave of his arms 'these stables.' There was such incredible hurt in his voice, such torture. This was truly a man that had reached the end of the line. A man who was more than prepared to start firing off that rifle. 'While you were here, with me, learning everything I knew, she went at your father with a knife. She cut his face from lip to ear. The next day he left for Ireland and she got news of his accident a week later.'

'My mother would never have done that. She didn't know how to be violent.'

'She had nobody left. You were too young to understand what had happened, you loved your father too much to be told the truth. I was all she had. I looked after you both. I nearly lost my wife.'

'You're lying. My father went back to Ireland because he knew what you were. Your wife knew too, that's why she opened up her wrists in the bath. She couldn't bear to go on living, knowing what you are. You ruined all of our lives, now you've ruined your own.' Nathan struggled to rise. 'And you deserve this,' he said. 'You deserve everything you get.'

Suddenly, faster than Nathan had expected, Corelli sprang forwards and pounded the butt of his rifle into the jockey's chest. Nathan doubled up, hit the hard earth with a gasp of expelled air. 'Stay down,' Corelli suggested, and Nathan did.

'Now what?' Nathan wheezed. 'You kill me? First the father, now the son?'

'I never wanted to hurt you, Nathan. You were like my son, the son I never had. You were supposed to take this stable off me when I couldn't look after it any more. That was going to be my gift to you.'

'You could never be my father.'

'I never wanted to be him.'

Nathan wiped a hand across his lips and it came away bloody. He spat disgustedly. 'What did she ever see in you?' he said.

'Kindness. Something your father never gave her. Those letters I showed you, the letters your mother wrote to me, they proved that.'

'Those letters proved you were sleeping with my mother. They proved you were a liar and a coward. You two. . . Sleeping together, right under your wife's nose while she was ill.' Nathan grinned and their was pure malevolence in the action. 'I guess she took it really badly when she found out the truth.'

Corelli paced backwards and forwards frantically, tears squeezing from the corners of his eyes. 'I never meant to hurt anyone.' He looked at the gun in his shivering hands, then at Nathan, still curled on the floor. 'I never wanted to hurt anyone. Your mother needed my help and I loved her. Eventually she came to love me too. We didn't have a choice in the matter, we couldn't stop the way we felt.'

'Listen to yourself. You're pathetic.'

'I loved you too. I was glad when your father left.' He laughed sourly. 'I was ecstatic when I heard he'd blown himself to pieces. Your mother was better than he ever was and I never wanted you to grow up like him.'

'That wasn't your choice to make.'

'And I keep telling you, I never made that choice. He left you because your mother wasn't prepared to cower when he walked in the room anymore.'

'There's more to it than that. You were always at the heart of it. Always there.' Nathan pulled himself back into a sitting position. His ear, where Corelli's initial blow had landed, was pounding like the side of his face was being panel-beaten into shape. If his hearing had been impaired from the attack he wouldn't be able to race again. The thought added fresh fuel to his uncompromising anger. 'You must have been behind it.'

Corelli thought for a moment, running one hand along the barrel of the rifle. 'Do you know why I showed you the letters?' he asked.

'Enlighten me.'

'When your mother died, you seemed so alone. I thought if you knew the truth you wouldn't be so cold. I thought you would see me as your family. I had no intentions of hurting you.'

'Then you seriously miscalculated the results of your actions.'

'I was so distanced from my wife by then, I was as lonely as you were. Then Charlotte's depression set in and she did that. . . that terrible thing with the razor, in the bath. I thought we could be there for each other.'

'One happy dysfunctional family?'

Corelli sat, letting his head hang. 'Maybe. I don't know. Maybe I felt some kind of responsibility towards you after everything I had been through with your mother. Does it matter?'

'It was my life.'

'I got the timing wrong. I should have given you a chance to come to terms with her death before letting you know the truth.'

Nathan glared and there was more than anger burning in his eyes. 'You never should have told me at all. Don't you understand that? My father killed eleven people with a bomb he made in the shed and my mother was a slut who couldn't stay off her back. Do you really think I wanted to know those things? Do you have any idea how lonely I felt after you told me those things?'

'I never thought.'

'You took my memories of them, Corelli. My dreams. You took away the only part of them I still had. And that's all you can say? You never thought?'

'I wanted to help.'

'You helped.' Nathan was standing. The ground undulated beneath his feet sickeningly. The world expanded and contracted with his every shuddering breath. 'You helped me hate, helped me not care anymore. You can't trust anybody in this life, nobody except yourself. You helped me realise that.'

'I'm sorry.'

'Sorry doesn't cut it anymore.'

Corelli looked up and his face was a mask of unquestionable pain. He had shaken the very foundations of Nathan's life and brought the world crumbling in without even realising. He was realising now. 'How do I get out of this?' he asked.

'You don't get out of this. You're too far in to ever get out again.' Nathan took a step nearer on uncertain legs.

'I think you're right,' Corelli whispered.

'Is it really all gone?'

Corelli rested the rifle across his knees and blinked his eyes clear. 'Today was the last chance. I really thought you'd come through for me.'

'Why?'

'I'm just an old fool, but I thought you at least owed me something. In spite of all the bad things.'

'And this?' Nathan flicked his head towards the stables. There was huffing and sneezing from the dark confines, the last of the horses making their presence known. 'This is all gone?'

'Everything.'

Nathan's laughter echoed in the still night. 'That's rich. That's just perfect. So was it worth it? Was your betrayal worth all this pain?'

'Even knowing what I know now, I can't feel regret for the time I spent with your mother, only regret for the people I hurt along the way.'

Nathan took another step. Another. Never for one second taking his gaze away from the rifle. 'I'm going to go now,' he said, forcing his voice to remain level. 'You've got two choices. You can watch me leave, or you can shoot me in the back.'

Corelli nodded understandingly. 'I guessed it would come to that.'

Nathan smiled and managed to allow a modicum of kindness soften the edges of his bleeding mouth. 'So what's it going to be?'

'I was never going to kill you. You know I was never going to kill you.'

'It didn't feel that way.' Nathan touched his bruised cheek, looked across once more at the empty stables, so sad in the waxing moonlight. 'If it's any consolation, I never wanted to see you totally destroyed. I really was sorry to see Jacobson tumble today.'

'You better go.'

'Is that all you have to say?'

Corelli sighed heavily. 'You perpetuate it, you know? The misery. You've passed it on to Nina.'

Nathan barely flinched at the sound of her name. Nina. The girl whose hair he could still smell. Vanilla, without even the faintest trace of cigarette smoke from the party. 'I know.' Something stirred inside him momentarily, a sleeping emotion looking for escape. 'But then, why should the pain be mine alone?'

Nathan turned away, faltered, then started walking. A dozen steps, maybe less, and Corelli called out. He sounded totally broken, shattered irreparably, like a war veteran standing at the white, nameless graves of his fallen comrades. 'Are you going to call the police?' he asked.

Nathan looked back. 'Do I need to?'

'I think so.' Corelli's eyes were wide and staring. 'It's worse than you think.'

'Why?' Nathan started walking back, his pace quickening when he was close enough to see Corelli's white knuckles wrapped around the shivering rifle. 'What have you done?'

'I helped her,' Corelli said, hopelessly. 'I wanted to help her.'

'Corelli?'

'She asked me.'

Nathan crouched, looking Corelli in the eyes. Fear. Pain. A dreadful, unspoken realisation. 'Who asked?' he said.

'Charlotte, my wife. She wanted my help. She said she wanted to go back.'

'Back where?'

'Just back. I helped her go.'

'Go where, Corelli?'

'I ran the bath.'

For a second Nathan was floating hopelessly, then the world slammed in around him, crushing the oxygen from his lungs. 'Oh Jesus,' he said. 'Oh Jesus.' Another second, a second that seemed too long, and he was on his feet, running for the house, dark universe speeding past him. No security light. Corelli had planned it.

'Oh Jesus.'

Nathan heard the gunshot behind him, winced, but didn't stop. Didn't stop. Threw himself against the front door of the house, banging with his palms on the wood. No answer. No lights at the window. All the curtains closed. A shrouded tomb.

Corelli had planned it.

Nathan slammed his shoulder against the door, panic burning in his brain, jostling his senses. His breath was snatching, almost impossible. No keys. He didn't have any keys. Corelli had the keys. . . Corelli, with his hands wrapped around that gun and the barrel wedged up under his chin. Bloodied skull, staring white eyes. The horses kicking and braying in their stalls. The keys shining by his twitching foot.

'Oh, Jesus.'

Nathan ran around to the nearest window, tried it. Locked.

Everything was locked. Of course it was locked. Corelli had planned it. He didn't want anybody to be able to get in to Charlotte.

Lovely Charlotte. Hopeless, lost Charlotte.

Nathan looked around. Saw the stone planter with the dead flowers in it. Heaved it up, threw it. The world exploded in a myriad of shimmering glass pieces, then he was in the reception room. Slipped on the rug, glided through to the main hall, heading for the stairs. Running in the darkness, taking the steps two at a time. There was music playing. Roy Orbison. Roy Orbison playing on a scratchy forty-five in the master bedroom. The suicidals' music of choice.

He blasted through the doors into the bedroom. Stopped.

The old record span and warbled on the player. The bed had been made perfectly. The door to the en suite bathroom was closed.

'Oh, Jesus,' Nathan said. Corelli had run her a bath.

The record popped and crackled, Nathan moved mechanically towards the bathroom door. He didn't want to go in. Didn't want to see Charlotte - kind, loving, wonderful Charlotte - floating in red water, head tipped back, eyes staring at the ceiling. Didn't want to see the jagged red scores across her wrists. Didn't want to see her lying there.

He took deep, swallowing breaths.

Opened the door.

For a moment the world, the universe, life itself, stopped. Nathan's tongue jammed in his throat. He had expected blood, but there was no blood here.

Corelli had done more than help.

Nathan staggered, grabbed the doorframe for support. It was no good, his legs disappeared and he slumped against the bed.

Then there was only flashing lights, sirens, uniforms and blank faces.

Chapter Nine

For a moment Nathan looked up into the glaring overhead light, then his eyes were drawn back to the slightly-overweight woman sitting across the table from him who had introduced herself as Detective Inspector Marshall. She was watching him suspiciously, one arm draped over the back of her chair. Her face - beautiful in a hard, perfectly organised kind of way - had been cut from a block of ice and her skill as a poker player was surely unsurpassed. As strange as it seemed, Nathan liked her, at least, as much as it was possible to like the woman who was attempting to make you confess to a double-homicide.

Behind her, on a smaller table, a tape recorder hissed quietly, recording the silence. A quiet, young officer with a five o'clock shadow stood by the door with his hands behind his back. He gave the impression of being slightly uncomfortable, perhaps slightly bored.

Nathan leaned back, allowing the stiff, wooden chair to creak its protest.

'Any chance I could get a coffee?' he asked.

Detective Inspector Marshall shot the officer at the door a quick nod, and after a moment of quiet, indignant outrage, the officer exited the room. DI Marshall, who was tired, overworked, and currently going through a messy divorce involving three kids who were at the age when they knew what the fighting meant, turned back to Nathan with a thunderous crease in her brow. 'Okay, Mr O'Donnell. The coffee has been ordered, the caviar will be through shortly. I have much better things to be doing other than talking to you, so let's get this parade started, shall we?'

'You can call me Nathan.'

'I'll stick with Mr O'Donnell if it's all the same.'

'Your call.'

Marshall smiled quick-wittedly. 'Yes,' she said. 'Let's start with your call.' She dropped a ring bound notepad on the table and flicked through a few well-thumbed pages. 'You rang us as soon as you found the body of Charlotte Corelli, is that correct?'

'Yes. . . No. No. For a while I just sat there on the bedroom floor. I couldn't think straight. I've never seen anything like that before.'

'How long?'

'Sorry?'

'How long did you sit on the floor for?'

'I don't know. Ten minutes? I wasn't exactly thinking straight at that time.'

'Ten minutes seems a long time to sit in close proximity to a dead body.'

'I couldn't feel my legs. I was shocked. It wasn't what I expected.'

'What you expected?' Marshall raised an eyebrow questioningly. The door opened and the young officer reappeared with a paper cup. He placed it in front of Nathan who looked at it with the same kind of suspicion that Marshall had reserved for him.

'Yes,' Nathan said. 'It wasn't what I expected.' He sampled the coffee. 'You put sugar in this.'

'And what were you expecting?' Marshall pressed.

'I was expecting a woman who had cut herself to pieces in the bath, I wasn't expecting to see a woman that had been held under the water until she stopped thrashing.'

'Colourful description. Did she?'

'Did she what?'

'Thrash.'

'Maybe. There was a lot of water on the floor.'

'Very observant of you to notice the state of the floor when there was a body floating face down in the bath.'

'I'm a jockey, being observant comes with the territory. Besides, I had plenty of time to wait around for your boys to show.'

'Indeed.' She referred to her notepad again. 'So you phoned around about one-thirty in the morning. Is that correct?'

'You're the one with the notepad.'

'You know, you come across as rather unhelpful. Should I be reading something into that?'

Nathan sipped his coffee. 'I had a huge race yesterday and I haven't slept since. I am drinking some of the worst coffee I have ever had the misfortune to ingest and two people I know are dead. You must forgive me if I'm a little out of sorts.'

'Okay. So you rang us about one-thirty. Want to tell us why you were out at the stables at that time of night?'

'I thought we'd been over this,' Nathan said, stifling a yawn.

'Lets go over it again.'

'Fine. It's your party.'

'Oh yes, the party. I understand you left early.'

Nathan frowned in puzzlement. 'Who told you that?'

'That doesn't matter. Did you leave the party early or not?'

'Not really. There wasn't much of a party left by the time I headed back to my cottage.'

'And what time was that?'

'I don't know, maybe eleven thirty. Maybe earlier.'

'That sounds early to me.'

'But you don't have to get up at six in the morning to train a string of colts over jumps, do you? Being tired in charge of a horse isn't advisable.'

'Really?' That questioning eyebrow again, arced with intrigue.

'People die on the gallops.'

'Yet, instead of going to bed in order to be bright and fresh for the morning exercises, you drove over to Barrowdown Stables?'

'I had a message from Corelli.'

'Yes, a message from a man you openly despised and refused to ride for. You got a message which, I am led to believe, you have since deleted from your answer phone, and let's not forget that the phone itself was subsequently smashed during Corelli's alleged assault on you.'

'I'm very thorough.'

'So you got this message and you just had to rush over to the stables in the middle of the night? You have to admit, that does sound a little bit strange.'

'He sounded distressed.'

'And you cared?'

'I don't know. A lot of things happened between Corelli and I, but he was still the trainer that got me started. I think I thought I owed him a few minutes of my time.'

'And it couldn't wait until the morning?'

'It didn't sound like it.'

'He must have sounded terrible. Distressed. Angry.'

'He did.' Nathan gulped the coffee now. His demeanour was relaxed, but inside his stomach knotted and bunched with every answer to every leading question. 'He also sounded drunk.'

'Yet you weren't worried what he might do if you went to see him?'

'I was worried about what he would do if I didn't. I had already been told he. . .' Nathan bit his tongue, but it was too late.

'Told what, Mr O'Donnell?'

'I had already been told he was losing his stables and he thought I was responsible in some way.'

'Really?' Pages flipped in the notepad. Nathan waited patiently. 'That is interesting. Who told you this?'

'Nobody.'

'Nobody?'

'There was a dance the other week. Corelli's business was getting powdered by the rumour mill. You overhear these things.'

'You said you were told.'

Nathan raised his paper cup. 'You said this was coffee. Guess we were both mistaken.'

'You do realise that even if you didn't do this, we could book you for wasting police time.'

'You don't need any help in that department Detective. You're wasting it all by yourself.'

'Okay. So you got this message and decided to go over to the stables. In order to. . ?'

'To see if there was anything I could do to help.'

'Right. Then what happened?'

'Look at my face.' Nathan turned his bruised cheek towards Marshall. 'What do you think happened?'

'I'll tell you what I think happened. I think you went over to the house because you knew Corelli was drunk. I think you wanted him to stop telling everybody that his business was sinking and it was all your fault. Bad press is just plain bad, isn't it?'

'His business was going down because he couldn't get winners. That was nothing to do with me.'

'Then, when you got there, you found Mrs Corelli instead. You spoke together. She demanded you leave the property. You refused, then, when she threatened to phone the police, you panicked. You weren't on the best of terms and she could tell them anything, couldn't she? How could you explain why you were at the stables that late? So, you dragged her up to the bathroom and forced her head under the water.'

'Stopping to pop on a little Roy Orbison on the way,' Nathan grinned.

'You held her under until she stopped moving,' Marshall pressed on. 'Then, as you were leaving, Mr Corelli came back and attacked you with his rifle. But you were stronger than he was and you wrestled the gun from him, pressing it up into his mouth and pulling the trigger. Tell me if I'm getting warm.'

Nathan put his hands behind his head. 'You have a very vivid imagination, Detective.'

'If I'm wrong, then tell me what did happen.'

'I've told you. I was walking up to the house when Corelli. . . Mr Corelli, hit me with what I'm guessing was the rifle. We talked for a long time, he threatened to kill me for ruining his trade.'

'It must have been scary.'

'I was too angry to be scared. I'd chosen to get on with my life, I couldn't understand why Mr Corelli wasn't able to do the same.'

'You'd chosen to get on with your life?' A ruffle of pages in the notepad. The scratch of a ball point pen over the whisper of the tape recorder.

Nathan swallowed. 'Eventually he decided to let me go, but not until he'd told me what he'd done.'

'He told you he'd drowned his wife?'

'Yes. No. He told me he'd helped her.'

'Helped her?'

'Helped her to die. She'd tried to kill herself before but Corelli had found her in time. She spent some time in a psychiatric hospital. The problem was she hadn't been crying out for help, she hadn't wanted to be saved. She had really wanted to die.'

'Why?'

Nathan paused thoughtfully. 'I don't know.'

'I think you're lying.'

'Think what you want.'

'What I think can go a long way in court.'

'I'm sure it can. Shame it doesn't go a long way in getting me a decent cup of coffee.'

Marshall leaned forwards, her eyes narrowing alarmingly. 'What are you hiding from me, Mr O'Donnell?'

'Nothing.'

'Why did Mrs Corelli want to die? Was it something Mr Corelli had done?'

'Why should I know?'

'Because you used to work for him.' Marshall's smile widened violently. 'As did your mother.' This was obviously some cue for the young officer because at the very mention of Nathan's mother he produced a clear plastic bag which he handed to Marshall. She placed it on the table.

Nathan looked at it.

'For the tape,' Marshall said 'Mr O'Donnell is being shown article seven, a letter written by Mrs Sinead O'Donnell. I think, Mr O'Donnell, you know who this letter was written to.'

'Where did you find that?

'Mr O'Donnell, let's stop playing games here. Tell me what happened last night.'

'I've told you.'

'Was Mrs Corelli institutionalised because she attempted to end her life after discovering her husband was having an affair with your mother?'

'Maybe. Who knows?'

'Is it the case that you left Mr Corelli's employment because of this affair?'

'That's true.'

'And is it true that you resented him ever since for what he did?'

'Give the girl a gold star.'

Marshall sprang up, smashing her palms on the table. The young officer by the door jumped then, looking slightly embarrassed, pretended to pick at some fluff on his jacket. 'Mr O'Donnell. You may be a big star in the racing community, but right now nobody gives a damn how good you are on a horse and you are in some serious trouble. Start giving me the answers I'm looking for or things could get very bad for you very quickly.'

Nathan's beaming smile grew brighter. 'You're gorgeous when you're angry,' he said.

Marshall laughed hopelessly. 'Why are you this way, Mr O'Donnell? What was it that damaged you so badly? These people have died, doesn't that upset you? You lived with them once, worked with them. Doesn't that mean anything to you?'

'Should it? What Corelli did while he was alive was no concern of mine. Should I care now because he drowned his wife and then blew his brains out?'

'Is that what you think happened?'

'That is what happened.'

'How can you be so certain of that?' Marshall sat, folding her hands neatly on the tabletop. 'Did you see what happened?'

'No.'

'But you sound so certain.'

'You didn't see the state Corelli was in.'

'I saw the state he was in afterwards. It takes a lot of guts to kill yourself. Do you think Corelli was strong enough for that?'

'I guess he must have been.'

'Well I'm not buying it.' Marshall picked up the clear plastic bag and shook it. The folded paper inside the bag bounced around fitfully. 'This letter makes it difficult to believe you would ever go to the stables to do anything other than harm Mr Corelli. I think,' again she leaned closer, conspiratorially, 'you killed them. Is that really what happened?'

Nathan let a hard laugh machinegun between his grinning teeth. 'You really are grasping at straws, aren't you?'

'Am I?'

'I never hurt them.'

'I don't believe you. I think you were angry with Mr Corelli. You knew he was in trouble and you wanted to go to him and completely break him, make him suffer for this.' She threw the letter at Nathan. 'You blamed him for taking your mother away, the only woman you ever thought you could trust.'

'You're a psychiatrist now?'

'I can see what you are, Mr O'Donnell. I don't need to be a psychiatrist to see you have a problem with women, especially authority figures,' her grin matched Nathan's in intensity, 'like me.'

'Do you think I'm scared of you?'

'I didn't say that, but I think when you found out about the affair your mother was having with Mr Corelli, something inside you broke. I think the part of you that could be human just fell out and left a bitter, young man with a deep and growing urge to seek revenge against the man who had taken his dreams away. Nobody likes to find out their parents are just people.'

Nathan steepled his hands before his chin. 'And you think I killed them because of that?'

'Maybe. Maybe you wanted to take away the woman Mr Corelli loved so that he could feel as empty as you do. How does that sound?'

'Like a book I read once.'

'The problem was you waited around too long and Mr Corelli came back, didn't he? He saw his wife, lying there in the bath, and he came after you with his gun. He chased you out to the stables where you surprised him and took the rifle. You shot him. Maybe you didn't want to. Maybe that had never been the plan, but you shot him anyway. Tell me that isn't true.'

'I never killed anyone.' Nathan drank the rest of his coffee and crushed the paper cup in his left hand. 'I doubt you can say the same for this coffee.'

Marshall sighed and referred back to her notebook agitatedly. 'Okay, Mr O'Donnell,' she said. 'If you didn't do it, tell me what happened after Mr Corelli knocked you down.'

'Christ.' Nathan flew up, his chair clattering behind him. 'How many times do you want me to tell you this? How many times is it going to take to make you realise my story is the same every time?'

'What's the matter, Mr O'Donnell? Not enjoying your little game anymore?'

Nathan chuckled, thought about it, retrieved his chair and sat. 'I can play this game all day if I have to.'

'Then you are playing games?'

'Your words, Detective.'

'Then give me some words of your own, tell me something that's going to get you out of this situation.'

'I don't need to.'

'Why?'

'Because I didn't do it.'

'I hear people saying that every day. Do you know how many I believe?'

'I can guess.'

'What you need to do is convince me. Tell me what happened after you arrived at the house.'

'This is absurd.'

'People lost their lives. Is that absurd?'

'Okay. It's like I've said before. Mr Corelli had taken out the security light.'

'Why?'

'I'm assuming it was so I wouldn't see him coming. I don't know. But he hit me and I blacked out. When I woke up he was waving that bloody gun around and acting crazy. He'd been drinking.'

'I was told Mr Corelli had a drink problem. Is that true?'

'Who told you that?'

'In this job it pays to have a lot of little birds.'

'They should be careful. Little birds have a tendency to get themselves shot.'

'Answer the question, Mr O'Donnell.'

'He was an alcoholic. He'd been dry since his wife came out of the hospital.'

'But he'd been drinking that night?'

'It was one of the reasons I went over there. I could tell from the message he left on my phone, he'd been drinking. I was worried he might do something he would regret.'

'So he'd been drinking and he hit you.' More notes were scribbled in the notepad. The same tired sentences over and over again. Always leading back to the same conclusion. 'What happened then?'

'We talked. He was venting some feelings, there was an argument.'

'I can't believe you would argue with a man who had already attacked you and was now holding you hostage at gunpoint.'

Nathan slouched further into his chair, rapping his fingers on the table. 'But to be honest, you don't really know me,' he said.

Marshall sighed exaggeratedly and motioned for Nathan to continue with a twirl of her hand. The officer at the door stifled a yawn.

'We talked for a while and eventually he decided to let me go. As I was leaving he told me about Charlotte and that was when I ran up to the house. The door was locked so I smashed the window.'

'Couldn't you have used Mr Corelli's keys to get in?'

Nathan grimaced, allowed his eyes to close. His throat worked rapidly. 'I didn't want to go back once I'd got that far.'

'Because?'

'Because I'd heard the rifle go off and I knew what he'd done.'

'So you broke the window?'

'Yes.'

'The window was broken after they were both dead?'

'Yes.'

'How do you know that?'

Nathan shook his head hopelessly. 'Would you just quit with that. I'd heard the gun go off, I'd heard the tremor in Corelli's voice when he told me about Charlotte. I just knew they were both already dead. It wasn't exactly rocket science to figure out.'

'So you broke the window, knowing Mrs Corelli was already dead?'

'Yes.'

'Why would you do that?'

'I . . . I don't know. Maybe I thought there was a chance she wasn't. Maybe I was hoping I'd be in time to help her.'

'Help. I keep hearing you say that.' Marshall stood and paced around the table so that she was standing at Nathan's back. She leaned down next to his ear, speaking softly. 'You say Mr Corelli said he had helped his wife, you say you wanted to help Mr Corelli.' Her breathing was calm and deliberate. 'What, exactly, is your interpretation of help, Mr O'Donnell?'

'The same as yours.'

'I think, perhaps, you broke that window in order to kill Mrs Corelli. I don't think you had any intentions of doing anything to help anyone when you turned up at the stables last night.'

'You're entitled to your opinion.'

'This could be very serious for you, Mr O'Donnell.'

'I doubt it.'

'Really? Why's that?'

'Because sooner or later some forensic boys are going to dust down that rifle and bits of fabric off Charlotte's body and you're going to realise I had nothing to do with either death.'

'Fine.' Marshall moved back so that she was standing in front of Nathan. She purposefully gathered up her notepad and tucked it into the pocket of her jacket. 'Interview terminated at two-thirty-five.' She hit stop on the tape recorder and the small room was filled with a deafening silence. It lingered uncomfortably for several moments before Marshall chose to break it. 'Maybe you didn't kill these people, but don't think for one second you didn't have anything to do with their deaths.'

Nathan's mocking smile flickered, dropped away. 'I went to help him,' he said.

Marshall turned to leave. 'Perhaps you should have done that earlier,' she said.

Chapter Ten

The first note appeared two months after the shooting incident and, after that, they arrived at irregular intervals.

They were usually - at least, in those initial few weeks - stuck under the windscreen wiper of his Jag', although eventually they would start appearing pretty much anywhere. Each one - jumbled letters cut from a newspaper and glued roughly into spitting, venomous sentences - was as horrifying as the last, but it was always the first Nathan would remember.

Die, it had said. Simply that. With no indication as to why. Just Die. And perhaps that was what made Nathan think this might be something more serious than the death threats he had received in the past. Perhaps it was the pure evil of that one word, the seeming randomness, the lack of any kind of motive or logical reasoning. Perhaps it was that the author of the note did not even feel the need to justify his need for Nathan's death, that the author did not care enough about his intended victim to waste his time finding more letters in the newspaper. Or perhaps it was just the way in which that one word cast such a suffocating shadow over Nathan's last few months on earth. Just that one little word.

Die.

*

Nathan looked at himself, in the bedroom mirror, then at the hump of bedclothes behind him. Another night, another girl. This was one of Lampar's own and, if the old trainer found out, there would be some awkward moments ahead. Lampar didn't like ripples in the water.

Lampar should never have employed Nathan if that was the case.

The hump groaned and rolled over. A pale, thin arm dropped out of the edge of the bed, rough fingernails tucked in towards the rough palm. A curl of long, brown hair swept out the top of the duvet and spilled over the pillows in which a face had been buried. There was an empty red wine bottle on the bedside table. There was another empty bottle downstairs.

Nathan drew his gaze away. The girl would need to be woken up. She would probably want coffee. She would probably want a promise he would phone. Same old routine.

'What do you think?' he asked his reflection. Dark eyes, his eyes, stared out at him from beyond the glass. There was no response. 'That's pretty much what I figured you'd say.'

The hump - it was definitely Lucy, he could remember hearing somebody call it Lucy - moved again. He thought about waking it up, decided against it and went down into the kitchen.

First, the percolator. Coffee spluttered and hacked as he moved around the kitchen, drawing curtains to allow the streaming sun to tumble over his cabinets and tables. Yellow light sloshed around the murky corners of the room and into the hallway beyond. Cups chinked as he removed them from a cupboard over the refrigerator. Two cups, he noticed. He had picked out two cups.

He checked the bread bin, rammed two slices of bread in the toaster and switched it on. The coffee finished bubbling and he poured. There was no movement from upstairs. He decided to keep it that way for the time being. He was feeling too delicate for any kind of disruption to his morning regime, least of all an awkward girl making demands.

He ate the toast dry, drank both cups of coffee and stepped outside to smoke his first cigarette of the day - a far simpler pleasure than the one sleeping in his bed.

Cold wind dragged noisily through the barren trees, rattling their skeletal branches together. There was rain in the air, distant black clouds rolling in from the south. The world was fresh.

'Look what you're missing, Corelli,' Nathan whispered, cupping his hands around the flicker of his lighter. The cigarette sparked and he swallowed back smoke, felt it spilling into his lungs. 'You could have got by. You always got by before.'

A huge crow settled in one of the nearest trees and watched him intently, its shoulders hunched and neck craned forwards for the best possible view. Two more crows were circling above Lampar's manor. The black claws of the coming rain inched across the butterscotch sky like an ink stain.

Nathan smoked his cigarette down to the butt and then stubbed it out on the cottage wall. The smoke he had inhaled floated in the huge expanse of emptiness he felt in his gut.

'Corelli.'

The police had been able to piece together the events of two months previous easily enough. Corelli's own stable hands confirmed that he'd been drinking and had sent them all home early. Fibres from Corelli's jacket had been found on Charlotte's skin and on the bath. The forensics team confirmed there had been no struggle, despite the excess of water on the bathroom floor, and there were no signs that she had been unconscious prior to being put in the bath. The trajectory of the bullet that had exploded out of Corelli's skull was consistent with him having put the gun in his own mouth. The rifle, bloody and stinking, had still been in his hand when they found him. There were no charges laid against Nathan, yet somehow that just seemed to make things worse.

He lit another cigarette and drew as hard as he could. Fat droplets of rain spattered on his hands and neck. The crow watched.

After it was all finished with, Nathan had taken a month off. He had not found the courage to go to the funeral and had instead hopped across the water to Ireland where he spent time getting reacquainted with some of his more welcoming relatives. His Aunt Maire had seen it all on the news and thought it 'a very bad thing', a 'terrible, terrible waste of human life'. Nathan could not fault her logic there.

He had been back two days now, and his first race was coming up in a week. The horse was an old nag with more wobble in her legs than bounce, but Nathan was happy to spend some time contesting races that were not going to put his face back on the front of the newspapers too soon. Glen Lampar supported him totally and had brought on a suitable replacement for the next few weeks, the ever-popular, if not ever-lucky, Neil Jacobson.

Nathan shuddered. The hole inside him gaped wider. 'When does it stop?' he asked. The crow cawed forlornly. It was only another moment and then the rain was falling in heavy, flat sheets. The sun continued to glimmer blearily in the watery haze.

Nathan lost the cigarette with a casual flick, sighed, turned back to the house. Rainwater dribbled curious rivers down his back and neck. For reasons he could not explain a name hung expectantly on his lips, waiting to be born. The name was Nina.

He went back inside.

She - the lump - was sitting at the kitchen table. She was wearing his dressing gown and had drained the remnants of the coffee percolator. She yawned and waved as he walked in and sat next to her. It was almost a minute before she finally said anything.

'That was fun.'

'Fun. Yes.'

Ugly word. Fun. This had never been about fun. This hadn't even been about sex.

'Rain again?' the girl asked, nodding towards the streaming window.

'We can use it. Been too dry around here lately.'

'Talking shop?' The girl - call her Lucy, it had to be Lucy - sipped her coffee. Steam curled languidly round her uninteresting mouth.

'What would you rather talk about?'

'Maybe there isn't anything for us to talk about.'

'Probably.'

The silence crowded in inquisitively. Nathan contemplated the empty percolator thoughtfully. Lucy chewed her bottom lip between sips of coffee. The rain slashed at the window.

'How long have you been with the stable now?' Nathan asked.

'Coming up to a year now.'

'Enjoying it?'

Lucy laughed and Nathan was flooded with anger at its mocking tone. She stood. 'Know what, I think I'm just going to leave. Thanks for the coffee and the. . .' she gestured 'other stuff.'

'Leave?'

'Yes, it's where I don't stay.'

'Right.'

She moved through to the hallway, Nathan followed stupidly. 'You don't have to go right away,' he said. 'You can finish your coffee.'

'I'm just going to get dressed.' She pointed at the stairs.

'Right.'

He watched her wiggle up to the bedroom door. Ten minutes later he watched her wiggle out of the front door. As she left, she looked over her shoulder. 'I'll call you,' she said.

Nathan leaned against the doorframe. Lucy disappeared down the lane and, just before she bobbed behind a bank of trees, he was almost completely overwhelmed with the urge to chase after her. What he would have done had he succumbed to that urge, he didn't know. 'Well, would you look at that,' he said, by way of an explanation. 'She can come again.'

There was a questioning caw from the treetops. The crow was still perched up there, a dark sentinel, black eyes glaring. In some cultures the crow was considered to be the bird of death, able to bring restless souls back to earth in an attempt to put right the things that had once been wrong.

Nathan shuddered unnecessarily.

Damned silly Hammer Horror nonsense.

There was a flap of wings and a second crow settled on the roof of his car. There was something else on the car too, tucked under one of the windscreen wipers. It flapped like a dismembered tongue.

An icy knuckle of fear wedged against Nathan's heart. He scanned his immediate surroundings for signs of any intruder. Nobody. Not even Lucy. He was totally alone. Just him, the crows, and that flapping thing caught under the wiper of his Jag'.

Involuntarily, his left foot took a step closer to the vehicle. The world rushed by him dizzyingly and suddenly he was reaching out, fingers touching the thing. Touching the thing that had not got caught under the wiper of his car by chance, but had been placed there carefully so that he would see it when he went out for his morning cigarette. If he had not been preoccupied, wouldn't he have noticed it so much sooner?

The rain hissed and rolled off the bonnet of the car, leaving shimmering patterns on the red paint. He unfolded the paper.

Die.

The note shook hideously in his trembling fingers.

Die.

Frantically, he looked over his shoulder. He was all at once encompassed by prying eyes, dark figures leering hungrily from every hidden recess. His heartbeat jacked against his ribs, thundering fear with every body-shuddering thud. The paper fell out of his hands and fluttered in the wind, skipping and dancing across the gravel before slapping against the side of one of the nearer trees.

Die.

The black clouds came tumbling from the sky and settled like a frozen slab in Nathan's stomach. His breath sharpened to a wheeze.

Die.

For minutes - terrible, endless minutes - Nathan thought he might.

Chapter Eleven

He burned the note. He probably shouldn't have done, but somehow he thought that with the word the grotesque feelings that were associated with it might also be burned and he could function normally once more.

It was hopeless. The word, such a small and insignificant word, formed a heavy punctuation to the life of careless abundance he enjoyed so freely and brought in its place a dark existence of constant worry and black doubts. He would never fully recover from the impact of that note, not even when confronted with the more explicit horrors of the letters still to come.

But for a fleeting moment, as he held his lighter beneath the damp, white paper and watched as it puffed into black smoke, he did feel better. He felt, possibly for the very last time, he was in control. Then he got the phone call from Lampar, asking him to come up to the house, and everything got worse.

He trudged through the rain, which was pouring down from the bustling clouds with an almost impossible vigour, with his head bowed and his hands thrust deep in overcoat pockets. As he walked, feet squelching in the grey rivers pouring down the gravel driveway, the names jostled around in his head. The possibilities.

Lord Cavanaugh? - perhaps suspecting that Nathan was the man who had been seeing to the overly-demanding needs of his wife? Then again, maybe not. It was over two months since Nathan had last seen Deirdre, and even the old lord, as drunk and stupid as he was, wouldn't have suspected anything after all this time. Besides, would he really care that much? An old man like that surely couldn't believe his wife was being faithful.

Terence Cavanaugh? - seeking some kind of revenge for being made to look a fool after Tiffany's Toast came in over the longer distance? Perhaps it was the humiliation of having his horse taken away from him. Or then again, maybe that was too absurd a reason. Maybe Terence was too much the lazy fop to bother with such a childish game as leaving crazy notes.

The Lady herself? - could Deirdre have left the note? The last time they had met, a week after Corelli had finally put an end to his business in the most brutally permanent kind of way, Nathan had told Deirdre he couldn't see her anymore, at least, not until he had found time to clear his head. She had not taken the news well, despite his protestations that it was only while he thought through all the mad things that were going on in his life. She had known better than that. He had been letting her go as easily as he knew how. Maybe that was enough to deserve a personal note.

He pushed his hands further into his pockets, ignoring the rain spilling over the collar of his jacket. Some of the second string horses were clumping around in one of the paddocks, two stable lads guiding them round on long reigns and trying to avoid the splashes from cantering hooves. Nathan waved at his colleagues as he passed and they waved back. He saw no faces.

Someone from Corelli's stables? Nathan shook his head. He would have pointed his finger squarely at Corelli if the old sod was still alive, but now he was dead. . . Nathan saw no reason to believe one of Corelli's disgruntled ex-employees would go to all the effort of hand-delivering a note of such ridiculous non-content. No. Most of the employees had found alternative employment. Nobody had liked Corelli enough to go to these lengths.

Then maybe it was one of Nathan's conquests; a girl who had not taken rejection too well? That seemed possible, there was a certain, silly, vindictiveness behind that note. It was the kind of thing a young girl might do out of spite. But really? Seriously?

Who knew?

Nathan reached the front door of the house and rang the bell, shaking droplets of rain from his hair. The door opened after a few seconds delay and he breezed through into the reception, shrugging off his coat and letting it drop on the tiles. The nameless, faceless, never-jobless maid that had answered the door, immediately picked the coat up and took it to a walk-in closet to dry. 'Mr Lampar is waiting in the dining room,' she said, without once looking directly at Nathan.

Nathan acknowledged the advice with a dip of his head and walked through to the dining room. His smile, which today was painted on a little thicker than normal, struggled to shine when he realised Lampar was not entirely on his own. A young girl, familiar in a gut-wrenching kind of way, was sat next to the trainer, talking excitedly. When Lampar saw Nathan standing in the doorway he motioned him in.

'Nathan, so good of you to stop by. Come in, dear boy. Come in.'

Nathan closed the door behind him, his eyes never straying from the girl for a second. 'Morning, Governor,' he said.

'Good to see the rain coming in. It's been too dry these last two months.'

'I was thinking the same thing,' Nathan said. Who was that girl?

'I knew you would be, and I know you'll be excited by what I've got to tell you. Sit down, please. Can I get you anything?'

'How's the –?'

'Coffee?' Lampar pointed to a cup on the dining table. 'Black, no sugar. You are nothing if not predictable. It'll kill you one day.'

'What? My predictability?'

'No, the coffee.'

'At least rigor mortis will never set in.'

Lampar grinned toothily. 'You in good spirits today, Nathan?'

Nathan glanced at the girl again, sampled the coffee, sat, cracked his knuckles. 'I don't know,' he said. 'What did you want to tell me?'

'Why beat around the bush when you can rip right through it, huh?'

'You're happy, Governor. It's too early for you to be drunk and you're too old to get laid. It always makes me nervous when you're happy.' Nathan's eyes narrowed as he examined the new girl, who still hadn't looked straight at him. Familiar girl; death threat. 'It's been an unusual morning,' he added.

'Okay, okay, I'll cut to the chase, but first, may I introduce the latest addition to the team. This is Nina.' The girl looked up and smiled sheepishly. 'Nina, I am sure you know Nathan.'

Like the floodgate to a nightmare had suddenly been opened, memories came hurtling at Nathan with such intensity his hands gripped around his coffee cup in a reflex action. 'New girl?' he managed, desperately wishing he had something funny to say but being let down by a brain instantaneously turned to mush by a wicked twist of circumstance.

'Pleased to meet you,' Nina said.

'New girl?' Nathan repeated. Christ. She didn't look anything like he remembered her. She looked. . . better, so much better.

'He'll be okay in a minute,' Lampar chuckled. 'He's had one or two tumbles in the past and his brain's a little more rattlely than it used to be.'

Nina extended a beautifully manicured hand for Nathan to shake. Not the hand of a stable lass. 'I'm looking forward to working with you,' she said.

Nathan accepted the hand. 'Working with me?' Nina's eyes widened playfully.

'Nina is going to be helping out around the stables. She comes highly recommended.'

'By who?'

Lampar shot Nathan an unimpressed glare. 'Is there a problem?' he asked.

Nathan released Nina's hand. 'You do realise where she used to work, don't you?' he asked.

'Do you have something you want to say, Nathan?' Lampar said.

Nathan looked from the trainer to Nina, then back over his shoulder. The rain drummed against the windows in harsh splatters. He had left the cottage empty, his Jag' parked unsuspectingly in the forecourt. He never locked that car, never locked that house. 'Actually,' he said, trying to keep his voice reasonably calm, 'I do have something to say. This girl used to work for Corelli. Remember him? He put a rifle in his mouth and blasted the top of his head halfway across Barrrowdown Stables. Do you remember that, Governor?'

Lampar sighed heavily. All the play had gone out of Nina's eyes. 'Nathan, you can't blame her for what Corelli did. She needs a job.'

'And that job has to be here?'

'Why shouldn't it be?'

Nathan bunched his hands on the table. 'Would you mind stepping out the room, Nina?' he asked, without risking looking at her again. 'I need to have a moment alone with the Governor.'

Nina stood. Lampar's hand shot out and held her wrist. 'No, Nina,' he said. 'This is my house and I say who stays and who goes. Whatever Nathan has to say, he can say it in front of you. Sit down.' He let go of her arm. She didn't sit. 'Nina?'

She looked at Nathan, who was glaring at Lampar from beneath his eyebrows. His knuckles were white. 'Maybe you need to talk alone,' she said.

'Good idea,' Nathan said.

'No,' Lampar insisted. 'We're just one big family here. I won't stand for this kind of unsightly behaviour. Nathan, apologise.'

'For what?'

Nina swallowed. 'Apologies aren't necessary. I need a breath of fresh air anyway.' She backed away from the table, eyes flickering between Nathan and Lampar. The air was charged. 'I'll wait outside.'

'Don't go too far,' Nathan said. 'Stay where somebody can see you.'

'Nathan?' Lampar's brow furrowed.

'Just do as I say,' Nathan snapped. Nina stepped away, glanced one more time at Lampar, who was clearly as shocked as she was, then left. Nathan's next breath visibly shuddered through his body, his hands flexed spastically. 'I don't trust her,' he said.

Lampar leaned back in his chair. 'What's got into you, Nathan?'

'She's one of Corelli's.'

'Not anymore.'

'Why are you bringing her on? We've got more than enough hands round here.'

'She's smart. Pretty too. I'm surprised you aren't all for it.'

'Under normal circumstances I might be.'

'Circumstances aren't normal?'

'It isn't the right time for this, Governor.'

'Why? What's wrong?'

Nathan began picking thoughtfully at his fingernails. His eyes remained down. 'I've slept with her,' he said. 'She was the girl I brought back from the Jockey's Fund dance.'

Lampar chuckled way back in his throat. 'You think I don't know that?'

'It could be awkward. I think she may have come here because of me.'

'She seemed smarter than that.'

'Since when have I been interested in smart girls?'

'I think you're more interested in her than you think you are. Maybe the problem isn't that she wants to be around you, maybe you're worried you want to be around her. It makes being a bastard so much more difficult when you start to feel things, doesn't it?'

'Way out, Governor. Corelli topping himself shook me up, I'll admit that, but don't think I've been through some kind of spiritual rejuvenation.'

'I don't. I think you've always cared more than you wanted to. I think that's probably why you hurt yourself so much.'

'Keep guessing. That girl out there doesn't mean anything more to me than the one I kicked out this morning. But I don't like the way she's just turned up here. I don't trust her.'

'She's hardly going to be selling information to Corelli, is she?'

'That's not what I mean.'

'Then what do you mean?'

Nathan's fingers clenched. He kept his gaze locked on the bottom of his coffee cup. 'Nothing,' he said, without conviction.

'Nina starts tomorrow. Go out there and congratulate her.'

Nathan stood. 'For the record,' he said. 'I consider this a very bad idea.'

'Noted,' Lampar said.

'Now, don't tell me you invited me up here just to tell me about the new stable hand.'

'Actually, no, I didn't. Tiff is up for a run before the end of the month and after what you did with her last time I thought it was only fair to offer you first refusal.'

'A month?'

'I know you wanted to stay out of the press for a while, but the opportunity's there. It's a Listed Race. Chance to get some black type.'

Black type: the bold ink used in an auction catalogue to reflect a prestigious win for the horse. A real chance to make Tiff, and all her offspring, soar in price. 'That's a very tempting offer,' Nathan said.

'Don't tell me now. Let me know.'

'I'll definitely think about it.'

'Good lad.'

Nathan stepped out of the dining room and pulled the doors closed behind him. Damn. That didn't go according to plan. He wiped a hand over his face, pressed his eyes closed. He should have told him. Why didn't he tell him?

'Nathan?'

He opened his eyes. He didn't even pretend to be pleased. 'Nina,' he said.

She was standing in the hallway, hands folded primly before her, hair flowing freely down over her shoulders in a way he would normally find quite appealing. Not today though. Not now.

'Congratulations,' he said. 'You got the job. You must be pleased.'

'You don't want me around here, do you?'

'Not especially.'

'Why not?'

Nathan crossed the distance between them in two strides and grabbed her arm forcefully. He dragged her to one side of the room. 'I think you know why,' he hissed, through gritted teeth. 'Did you think I wouldn't put two and two together?'

'I don't know what you mean.'

'The note.'

'Note?'

'Stop playing dumb.' His voice was hard and flat, like a sledgehammer.

'What note?'

'The note you left on my car this morning. What are you? Crazy?'

'I didn't leave any note.'

Nathan released her arm. 'Some coincidence. You turning up the same morning as I start getting love letters.'

'Love letters?' She looked genuinely confused. 'You're angry about love letters?'

'Not exactly.' The anger drained out of his voice and the straight line of his jaw, but the menace remained. The menace saturated every syllable, every twitch of his lips. 'Why did you come here?'

'I need a job. I haven't worked since Mr Corelli. . .' a troubled mixture of emotions lighted on her brow for the briefest of moments. Love, hate, sorrow. 'I thought I could be of use here.'

'Fine. Then welcome to the team.' He smiled viciously. 'But I warn you now, stay out of my way.'

'Okay.'

Nathan leaned closer so that his lips brushed against her ear as he spoke. 'If I see you so much as look at any of my rides, I will make sure you never work again. Do you understand?'

Nina could find no words. Nodded instead. That was okay.

Words weren't necessary.

Chapter Twelve

It - Nathan found it hard to bring himself to call it anything other than It - was much the same as the last one. Same kind of paper, same kind of type, folded in the same kind of way. Left in the same place, tucked under the windscreen wiper, and with a content almost entirely derived from pure, driven, undisclosed hatred.

I see you're emptiness. You didn't need to be cut to feel empty. Suffer.

Die.

Nathan screwed the note into a tight wad and threw It across the lounge. It hit the couch, bounced back and landed in the centre of the room. As he watched, from where he sat on the floor in the corner, It slowly began to unfurl like a white rose. He twisted his hands together agitatedly, felt the sweat creeping along the creases of his neck. The air was thick and cloying.

A second note. Somebody had gone to the effort of structuring a second note.

In the silence, Nathan's heart thudded blood in his ears. The whole world skittered in and out of focus with each laboured breath. He tried to force down the cold, terrifying emotion that was creeping through the coils of his intestines. This was nothing. A note. A thing. A silly game somebody was playing. Certainly not anything he should be worrying about. Nothing to cause a freezing vice to clamp around his trembling heart.

Nothing.

A second later and he had the phone in his hand. He pressed the receiver to his ear, stabbed out a number with palsied fingers.

'Governor,' he snapped.

'Nathan?'

'Is the new girl in today?'

'Sorry?'

'Nina. The new girl. Is she on the grounds today?'
'Of course. She's out on the gallops with Tiffany's Toast.'
'Tiff'?'
'What's this all about, Nathan?'
'You've let the new girl exercise Tiff? Is she supervised?'
'Of course. Nathan, are you okay?'
'No, I'm not okay, damn it. I told you not to bring her on staff. And now you're leaving her with Tiff. Jesus, what is wrong with you?'

There was a sigh on the other end of the line. 'Nathan, listen to yourself for a minute. I'm prepared to take only so much from you. I will not have you questioning the way in which I run my stables.'

'You can't leave Tiff with just anybody. She already has designated hands.'

'Are you going to tell me what all this is about?'

'I'll tell you what this is about. This is about letting people you hardly know come and work for you. She's not here because she needs a job, she's got a problem with me.'

'This sounds very much like paranoia, Nathan.'

'This is more serious than you know.'

'Are you sure this isn't more to do with control? You always did like to be in the driving seat, didn't you?'

'She got this job to be close to me. She came here to extract some kind of twisted revenge because I never got back to her after the party.'

'And, of course, you have proof of this.'

'I've got the proof right here.'

'What proo -?'

Nathan slammed the phone down. 'Damn you,' he hissed. 'Damn you.' His breathing was shallow and rasping. 'I'll deal with this myself. I'm not going to let this control my life.'

And around about the time he was telling himself that, something inside of him snapped. The part that kept him rational splintered and a sliver of it spiked into his brain. The fear poured out of his legs and an incredible fury spilled into the gap it left. He welcomed its hot, bubbling arrival.

New resolve strengthened his spine. He grabbed his jacket. Damned if he was going to sit in the corner and hide away from this. Damned if he was going to let It - It; only a note - destroy him.

He snatched the crumpled letter from where it had fallen and bolted for the front door. The heavy mist of a perfect winter morning billowed around him as he ran out across his driveway and headed for the gallops were Tiff' would be taking some light exercise.

'Hey,' he shouted, when he saw shapes looming out of the grey blanket of mist. 'Hey, you.' One of the shapes - Nina - turned to look at him, but from this distance it was impossible to see her face. A larger shape - Tiff' - bucked her head and stamped her hooves. There were other shapes too, other horses and trainers milling around, but nobody, nobody, was supervising Nina.

'You,' Nathan shouted as he approached, the scrunched paper mashed in one fist. 'I don't know what you think you're trying to achieve with this, but I'm telling you right now to stop it.'

'What's wrong?' Nina asked. Nathan furiously snatched Tiff's reigns away from Nina and thrust the note in Nina's face.

'This is wrong,' he said.

Nina cautiously took the paper and smoothed it out. Her eyes remained, disconcertingly enough, looking straight at Nathan.

'Care to explain this?' he asked.

She broke her stare, read the note, looked back. 'Somebody doesn't like you?' she tried.

'Or maybe somebody likes me too much.'

Nina glanced at the note again. 'That's not how I read it,' she said. 'The question is, why are you waving it under my nose. I'm assuming it was for some other reason than a second opinion.'

'I thought you might know how it managed to find its way on to my car.' Tiff' snorted disapprovingly. Nathan's grip on the horse's reigns tightened. Other shapes in the mist were looking at him, their shrouded faces no doubt wearing blank or confused expressions.

'I'm sorry,' Nina said. 'I can't help you. Is this like the letter you received the other day?'

'You know it is.'

'It wasn't from me.' Nina smiled, and though genuine enough, something behind that smile caused a ripple of fear to shiver the length of Nathan's spine.

'Then who was it from?'

'How should I know?' The smile widened. 'You really want it to be me, don't you?'

Nathan grabbed the note from her hand and stuffed it into his jacket pocket. 'I don't care who it is. I just want them to stop.'

'You do. You want it to be me. You want to think I'm all screwed up because you never phoned me. It makes you feel better, doesn't it? Poor little girl, stuck at home cutting her hatred out of the newspaper headlines? You want me to be hurting.'

'You're talking nonsense.' There was little conviction in his tone.

Nina reached over and removed the reigns from his hand. 'I don't think so. And I think whoever sent those notes knows you pretty well. You are empty. There's nothing in your heart.'

'You don't know what I have in my heart.'

'Exactly. And I wanted to, crazy as that might seem. I wanted to know.'

'You never called me.'

'But I waited for you. You were the one that wanted to be in control.'

'I. . .'

'Well, maybe it's time you weren't in control for once. Maybe you should be a pawn in someone else's little game.'

She turned without another word and led Tiff into the mist. Nathan watched until they were just two more shapes in a line of similar shapes.

He lowered his head. Perhaps it wasn't her.

'Then who?'

Somebody who knew him well. Somebody who had worked with him, perhaps slept with him. Somebody who felt bitter towards him, who could organise somebody else to leave the notes in case the deliverer was spotted. Somebody with a lot of spare time.

His head snapped up, his eyes widened. It could only be one person.

He was running again.

*

Before he was fully aware of what he was doing he was jamming his car keys into the ignition and backing out of the drive. The weighty vibration of the Jag' shivered a sense of control through his hands as the power-assisted steering nimbly carried him out on to the main road. He was in control.

He looked at his furious face in the rear view mirror. He was in control, damn it.

The road swished by, green and grey and brown. He rolled the window, let the wind rip at his collar, run its sharp, invisible fingers through his hair. This was being alive. This was what being alive was all about. Being in control, taking action.

He screamed, thumped his hands on the steering wheel. Cars shimmering by in the other direction were sardine tins filled with sardine families. Nervous drivers watched as he swerved untidily.

Control. Action.

He was always in control. He always had been in control. Nobody was going to take the control away from him. Not even Corelli, that incredibly pompous circus clown, had been able to do that. Nathan was the man. He was the controller.

He span the wheel hard, screeched into a tight bend and headed out towards open roads. The adrenaline throbbed behind his madly staring eyes.

The signs flashed by, white smears on the rapidly passing world.

He floored the accelerator, relishing the animalistic roar of the

Jag's motor. He was the driver. The car was his to control.

Like everything else.

Faster.

He was going to put an end to this, by God.

As the morning wore on, the mist dropped away until Nathan was driving through brilliant sunshine. The Cavanaugh residence loomed up on the horizon, imposing and dark against the brightness of the day. Nathan could almost imagine her, sitting up in one of the bedrooms, carefully selecting the letters for her next correspondence.

Lady Cavanaugh. The only person, when he really thought about it, with the time and inclination to extract such a tiny revenge.

He pulled into the driveway and cruised through the gardens. The stone gaze of the female-shaped fountain fixed him unnaturally as he pulled on the handbrake and got out of the car. The old butler had obviously seen him approaching and was standing at the front door expectantly.

'Hi, Lurch,' Nathan said. 'I need to speak to Deirdre.'

'Splendid, Sir,' the butler said, accepting Nathan's jacket as it was handed to him. 'If you would like to follow me through to the lounge.'

The butler headed off along the same route as when Nathan had last been at the house. Last time Nathan had been making efforts to gain control of Tiffany's Toast's entries and declarations. This time, he was trying to gain control of his life.

The butler walked quickly. Nathan followed. The same pictures lined the walls. The same smiling faces.

'So, how is Deirdre?' Nathan asked.

The butler snorted in a way that suggested even if he knew he was unlikely to say.

The butler. . .

Perhaps he was the one making the deliveries for Deirdre. Had he ever divulged his name? Would Nathan be able to describe him to a police officer if he was ever asked to?

Nathan tried to get a better look at the butler's face who, if anything, quickened his stride to ensure that no such look was possible.

'How long did you say you'd worked here?' Nathan ventured.

'Would Sir require a drink of any kind?' the butler said.

'Do you ever answer questions?'

The butler glanced over his shoulder. Said nothing.

'Everyone's a comedian.'

They reached the lounge door and the butler opened it, gesturing for Nathan to go in. It was obvious Lady Cavanaugh had seen him driving up to the house as she was already reclining beautifully, supporting her head with one delicate hand. She was wearing realistically comfortable trousers and a knitted sweater yet she managed to make the combination look delightfully elegant. Nathan took a seat opposite, without waiting for an invitation of any kind.

'Nathan,' Deirdre said, looking at him from under half-closed eyelids. 'So good to see you again, darling. I trust you're looking after my horse.'

'I'm looking forward to giving her a run next month.'

'Really?' The eyelids opened wider. 'I thought you were staying out of the limelight, running nags until your nerve came back.'

'Nothing to do with nerves. And where Tiff is concerned I'll make an exception. I earned the right to first refusal on that horse and I intend to run her when and where I get the chance.'

'You earned the right?' Deirdre repositioned her legs in a slightly more provocative way. 'Surely it wasn't that tough for you.'

'Granted. But there may have been some unforeseen repercussions.'

'Such as?'

Nathan glanced around the room as if to check they were totally alone. 'This,' he said, removing the scrappy note from his jacket pocket.

'What is it?' She took the note and read it. Her eyes widened alarmingly. She read the note again. 'Oh my goodness,' she said. There was a hanging silence so, for extra effect, she said it again. 'Oh my goodness. How terrible for you.'

'Terrible,' Nathan confirmed. 'You wouldn't happen to have sent this note, would you?'

'Oh my goodness.' This time there was some genuine emotion in the words. Some shock. 'You believe I would do something this cruel?'

'Why not? We hardly parted on civil terms, did we?'

She sat up, her back suddenly straight with indignation. There was nothing seductive about her in that instant. 'I can't believe this,' she spluttered. 'I can't believe you would even think that.'

'You have to admit, you are a likely suspect. The most likely, actually.'

'Well, how silly.' Deirdre relaxed slightly, letting some of the tension drain out of her shoulders. A careful smile played around the edge of her lips. 'You are, of course, joking. Either that or you have some evidence to substantiate such an incredibly slanderous' - the word rolled like treacle - 'remark. Do you have such evidence?'

The perfect line of Nathan's jaw remained resolute, his best poker face hiding the almighty-Christ of bad hands. 'You like to play games, don't you?' he said. 'You were playing when you slept with me. Telling me your husband knew about me even as we. . .' he waved the rest of the sentence away with a non-committal gesture. 'Just to see if I would still go through with it, I expect. To add a little more excitement.'

'I have no time for games, Nathan.'

'I would have thought you had more time than most. It must get so lonely in this big house, all day, by yourself.' He stood, walked around Deirdre's chair. His shoes clumped over the floorboards. 'The husband's away, you're a little bored. Why not while away the time cutting letters out of the newspaper?'

'I'd like you to leave now, Nathan.'

He leaned down next to her ear, vaguely aware that Detective Inspector Marshall had done something similar during his interrogation. An excited thrill coursed through his veins. 'I'm sure you'd love me to leave. Or, maybe you'd rather I didn't. Maybe you'd rather we went up to your room, did it in your husband's bed. Is that what you'd rather do?'

Suddenly the door sprang open and the butler appeared with a tea tray laden with silverware and a steaming jug. Wordlessly, he glided across the room, placed the tray on the nearest table to Deirdre, turned, walked back out. Nathan struggled to remember whether he had asked for any coffee.

'Very efficient, isn't he?' Nathan said.

'Well trained,' Deirdre said. 'Now, please get out of my house.'

Nathan straightened. 'Shame to let the coffee go to waste.' He moved around and poured two cups. Without asking, he added cream and sugar to one cup.

Nathan sipped the unsweetened coffee. It was better than what he was used to.

'Okay,' he said, trying on several different smiles before finding one that felt natural. 'If you didn't send the note, who did?'

'Should I know?'

'I think you may have an idea.'

'I don't.'

'What about your husband?'

'I very much doubt it.'

'You said he suspected you were seeing someone. Did he ever mention it?'

'No.'

'Do you think there's any way he could have figured out who it was?'

'I doubt it. My husband is very rich, he is not very clever.' She seemed somehow pleased with this. 'Besides, I doubt he would worry too much about it anyway. He's more concerned with his gold mines and whatnot.' Her grin stretched significantly. 'And he gets what he wants from me when he needs it.'

'That was the mental image I was looking for,' Nathan grimaced. 'You may just have put me off sex for the rest of my life.'

'Does that mean you're not mad at me anymore?'

Nathan set his coffee cup back on the tray. 'I'm mad at someone,' he said. 'But I don't think you sent me the letter. And I guess I have to take your word that your husband didn't know anything about me.'

'So what now?'

'Now I go back to the drawing board and think again.' He shook his head sadly. 'I don't know, it's all so crazy. It plays on my mind all the time. I think, if I just knew who it was, why they were sending me these things, I'd be okay. It wouldn't matter.'

'Have you upset someone recently?' Deirdre asked the question while interestedly scanning the letter again for further clues. 'Really upset someone?' she added.

'I have a tendency to upset lots of people, lots of the time. This isn't the first time I've received death threats.'

'It must be nice to be popular.'

'This is serious. Normally the threats are stupid and they normally come in with the fan mail. This note, and another note before it, were hand delivered. They were left on my car.'

'Really?'

'Somebody came into the stables and left the note on my car. That is serious. This whole damned situation is serious.'

'I agree.' Deirdre had resorted to her previously relaxed posture, her feet tucked up beneath her and her head tipped back to reveal the line of her elegant throat. 'It must be terrible to think that somebody dislikes you enough to hand deliver these notes.'

Nathan took the letter from her. 'It couldn't be Terence, could it?' he asked.

'Terence?' As much shock in the voice as when Nathan had suggested she, herself, had been the perpetrator of this terrible crime. 'Terence would never do anything like this.'

'Can you be certain of that?'

'What reason could he have?'

'I embarrassed him by coming to you and asking you to hand over the responsibility of Tiff's entries to Lampar. That kind of thing can weigh heavily on a young man's mind. He may hold a grudge against me.'

'But he would never be so foolish.'

'Pride is a foolish thing. You took back something you gave to him.'

'He knew the horse was never really his.'

'But you gave him the right to select what that horse did. That was power. You took that power away from him, and I was the reason why.'

'Even so.'

'Even so, I think I'd like to talk to your son.'

'Even so, he's in Africa at the moment with his father. Learning the business.'

'Point taken.'

Chapter Thirteen

Chepstow.

There was less flash and flare than there had been at Aintree, the races today were of less significance. However, a race was still a race and the excitement was tangible as the horses filed out along the rails.

But when he thought back to that day, the day that would actually put an end to his career as a professional jockey, all Nathan could remember was the phone number on a business card and somebody he didn't recognise tightening up the straps on his saddle before he mounted up.

All he could remember was. . .

'Nathan.'

His eyes narrowed as he strained to see across the length of the paddock. Gertrude, the chocolate filly he would be riding, was blustering noisily, over-excited by the attention and too skittish to have any chance of winning. She was braying and huffing, a sign she would fight against Nathan all the way down to the tape, losing the race even before the 'off'. Someone Nathan did not know threw on her weight cloth and saddle. A young lad, perhaps twenty. Had Lampar been taking on new staff again?

'Nathan O'Donnell.'

He was vaguely aware of somebody calling his name and a huge, rough hand clamped on his shoulder. He turned, almost screamed. A wide expanse of perfectly pressed suit towered over him.

Nathan stumbled backwards, the hand on his shoulder fell away, and for timeless moments he was certain, absolutely certain, the author of the notes had sought him out. Here, in the paddock at Chepstow, in the midst of hustling, bustling crowds, he was going to be murdered. He looked up into the hard, calculated face of his assailant. Waited.

'Mr O'Donnell,' the face said, and sunlight flared blindingly off designer sunglasses. No eyes. His murderer had no eyes.

'Yes?'

'My name's Christian Quigley. I've been looking for you.' One of those lump hammer hands reached inside the jacket. Nathan's stomach folded in half and his bowels loosened. Oh Christ. He was going to be shot, executed at point blank range.

White fingers of ice stabbed through his veins, his feet were welded in place, his throat contracted. He couldn't move, couldn't speak. He glance over at Gertrude. The unrecognised hand had disappeared and now Alicia, one of Lampar's regular staff, had the horse's reigns. She was stroking Gertrude's mane and looking around agitatedly for Nathan.

'I heard you've been having a spot of difficulties.'

Nathan looked back at the suit, then lifted his eyes up, up, to look at the man in it. A card was being held out for him to take. He took it, read it.

'Security?' he said.

Christian nodded and, when he did, Nathan caught a glimpse of coiled wire leading to a microphone ear piece. 'I look after people,' Christian said.

'You're a bodyguard?'

'Something like that.'

Nathan let a thin smile sketch a line in his mouth. 'You heard about the letters?'

'Word about this sort of thing has a habit of getting around.'

'And you think a few letters constitutes a need for personal security?'

'Would put your mind at ease. How many letters have you received?'

'The fourth came this morning.'

'In the mail?'

'Taped to my front door in a plastic wrapper.'

'Trust me, that constitutes a need for security. Most death threats are just idiot people venting steam. They send a letter off in the mail and that's an end to it. What you have is a genuine obsessive and that could be dangerous.'

'Obsessive?'

'He dislikes you so intensely he's prepared to personally make sure you receive every letter at the time he wants you to receive it.'

'He?'

'Or she. Any idea who it might be?'

'Could be anybody. I have a nasty habit of upsetting people.'

Christian nodded politely, in a way that suggested this was not entirely uncommon among his clients. 'Keep that card. It's got my direct number on it. Leave a message and a contact on the machine and I'll organise some protection for you.'

'I really don't think that's going to be necessary.'

'Keep the card anyway.'

Christian offered one of his giant hands and Nathan shook it.

'I'll keep you in mind.'

'Good luck out there today.'

Nathan headed across the paddock, fingering the business card thoughtfully before concealing it inside his vest. Alicia was visibly relieved to see him approaching.

'Mr O'Donnell, I was beginning to worry.'

'Hi, Sweetheart. How's the horse looking?'

'Excited. I'm sorry, I can't seem to get her to calm down.'

'As long as she jumps I'll deal with the rest.'

He mounted up and kicked away. He filed into position and made a canter down to the tape. Gertrude flicked her head and snorted and pulled and generally did everything within her power to ensure she was exhausted by the time Nathan had brought her to a stand.

At the start, secondary checks were made on the saddles in case the horses had blown up but Nathan was too preoccupied to pay attention as to who was doing the checking.

Then he was in the line up. Gertrude was already breathing heavily, stamping and chewing on her bit. She was going to be lucky to make it round the two mile run. She bellowed horribly. Christ, she was going to be lucky to make it over the first furlong.

Nathan took a deep breath. Two more. 'Please be calm,' he whispered.

Then the starting flag dropped and a wave of thoroughbred racehorses swept out onto the course. Gertrude took one stride, two strides. Nathan dipped in the saddle. Three strides, four strides. The world became a cacophony of drums and the squealing wind.

Five strides.

And then the saddle slipped.

Nathan felt it go suddenly, saw the line of the horizon tilt terrifyingly. Then the chewed earth was rushing towards him and his universe exploded in a shower of darkness.

As suddenly as that, Nathan's career was over.

Chapter Fourteen

Blurry, mainly white, cold and sterilised, the world began to slot back into place.

Firstly, there was light, and light was good. Light meant he was still alive. Then, growing with intensity like a dying star, there was the pain. For a while he had thought it was only in his right leg, a spike of fire that had been thrust through the bone of his knee, turning the cartilage to jelly. But, he realised soon enough, it wasn't just the knee. The pain was all encompassing, travelling in disorientating waves through his body.

For a while, the pain was all he could think about.

But even pain has to stop at some point, and there were other things vying for his attention. The smell of sterilisation, the distant, familiar voices, the beep beep beep of medical equipment.

Each new smell, each new sound, each new sensation, clicked into place like part of a jigsaw puzzle and slowly, surely, he began to piece together the tattered remnants of his life.

He opened his eyes.

White ceiling, white walls. Overhead halogen lamps, switched off. Flapping paisley curtains at an open window. Cool sheets. White. Soft pillows. Television mounted on a wall bracket, switched on, sound down. Black and white western. James Stewart and John Wayne. The undeniable stench of vomit, vaguely masked by swathes of sickening disinfectant.

And not alone. There was somebody sitting next to him. Someone familiar. Lampar.

Nathan's leg was in a cast and covered with a violent-looking medieval contraption. With dawning horror the pain came flashing back to the front of his mind. He pressed his eyes closed and waited for Lampar to say something, which, eventually, he did.

'Nathan.' Lampar's voice was cracked and frail, full of tiredness.

'Hello, Governor.' Nathan kept his eyes closed. If he opened them again he would see the metal skewered in his leg, the throbbing needles in his arms. He didn't want to see that. Seeing it made it real. 'How long have I been out?'

'Almost a week.'

'A week?' Nathan laughed feebly. 'Jesus Christ. What happened to me?'

'You died.'

Nathan's eyes flicked open. The beeping and hissing and pinging of the surrounding machines seemed to be even louder than before. Blood rushed in his head, stinging his brain.

On the television, James Stewart stuttered silently through his lines.

'What do you mean?' Nathan asked.

'There was a problem with your saddle, a fault. Nobody could have detected it, but the pressure of the race caused it to split.'

'Split?' Nathan rolled the word around. 'What are you talking about, Governor?'

'The saddle broke and slipped. You took a spill.' A pause, brief, but telling of how horrible that spill must have appeared to the crowds. 'It was a bad one. You came off in the middle of the field and at least two other horses hit you.'

'I don't remember.'

'You took a pretty bad blow to the head. There was some haemorrhaging.'

'My leg?'

'Totally shattered. There was some serious reconstruction work required. That wasn't the worst of it though. Some blood. . .' Lampar swallowed. 'Some blood on your brain needed draining. They say. . . That is to say. . . The doctors. . .'

Nathan sighed heavily and let his aching head sink back into the pillows. 'I'm never going to be able to race again, am I?'

Lampar touched Nathan's hand gently. 'They say another fall could kill you.'

Nathan stared at the ceiling. A tumble of thoughts jostled and argued in his head. 'You said I died,' he said.

'That's right.'

'What happened?'

'Your heart stopped while you were in the ambulance. They had to shock you so bad your chest burned.'

'How long was I gone?'

'A minute, maybe two.'

Two minutes.

Nathan tried to think. He could vaguely recollect a conversation he had been having with a stranger before mounting up. Then nothing. Just a vast expanse of darkness awaiting the hand of an onlooker to paint in the details he had missed. Missed because he was dead.

He had been dead. Perhaps he would have been better off if they had never revived him. Cold self-pity flooded his senses momentarily. What was the point in reviving him? What good was he if he couldn't be a jock?

'You'll be okay,' Lampar said, as if reading Nathan's mind. 'You'll make an almost full recovery, although they say you'll always have a slight limp. And the insurance will make sure you're well provided for until you can find other work.'

'And my home?'

Lampar exhaled slowly. 'Ah. Well, the cottage has always been reserved for the retained jockey. You would, of course, need to find alternative accommodation. Not immediately, of course. I wouldn't want to see you homeless.'

Nathan twisted his hands into knotted fists. 'And what am I supposed to do now?'

'You're a talented young man. There are plenty of opportunities out there for people like you.'

'But I'm a jockey,' Nathan growled. 'If I'm not a jockey, what am I?'

Lampar patted Nathan's shoulder. 'We are not always what we do. There is more to you than being a jockey. You could be a trainer with the eye you have for horses. There is always something else.'

'I need to ride.'

'Why? So you can continue having your photo in the paper?'

'Maybe.'

'Nathan, you're alive. This is a miracle. I have that race on tape and I can play it to you. You have no idea how badly hurt you were.'

'Bad enough to destroy my life.'

'Life? You call your existence a life? Racing and sleeping around with anyone who isn't brave enough to stand up to you when you start bullying them?'

'Are you condemning me?

'Do you know how many visitors you've had since your fall?'

Nathan closed his eyes and forced his hands to flatten on top of the bed sheets. 'I can guess.'

'Two, Nathan. Two visitors.'

'That's one more than I would have reckoned on.'

'Doesn't that say something to you? Doesn't it suggest you should change your lifestyle?'

'My lifestyle suits me.'

'But it doesn't suit anybody else. You could die a very lonely man.'

'Being lonely isn't so bad. Rather that than surrounding myself with liars.'

Lampar sat back and the hard chair creaked in protest. 'My, my,' he said. 'Corelli really did a number on you, didn't he?'

'And what does that mean?'

'It wasn't just Corelli, either, was it? Your father played a part, and your mother.'

'Don't talk about my mother.'

'Why not? Is this all a little too close to the mark for you?'

'You don't know what you're talking about.'

'You've got a self-destructive streak as wide as your father's was.'

'I am nothing like my father,' Nathan spat, through gritted teeth. He let out a shuddering breath. 'You should go.'

'You're probably right, but you should know, Nathan, just because you choose not to let anybody in, doesn't mean that people haven't found other ways to get close to you.'

'Which means?'

Lampar stood. 'Some people love you, Nathan, even if you won't let yourself love them. Even if what your mother did to you stopped you trying.'

Nathan chuckled unpleasantly, a cracked and pitiful laugh. 'You said two people have been to see me,' he said. 'Who was the second person?'

'Nina.'

'Nina from the stables?'

'I was surprised too. She's been sat with you most nights. She was holding your hand when you first came around.'

'I. . .' Nathan stared at the ceiling. 'I don't remember that.'

'She'll be in to see you later today. It would be nice if you could put aside whatever it is that's been troubling you when she does.'

'She's been with me all the time?'

'Mostly.'

'Did she say anything?'

'About what?'

'The. . . accident. Has she said anything about what happened?'

'Not to me.'

Nathan let his eyes flutter closed. The pillows were cool. The flap of the curtains at the window was almost hypnotic.

The. . .

Room. . .

Was. . .

'Nathan?'

His eyes sprang open. Someone was sitting beside him, talking through a nervous smile.

'Nina?' he said.

'No.' There was a twinge of hurt in the voice. 'No, it's Alicia.'

'Alicia?' Nathan struggled to sit forward. His broken leg was a knotted web of fire, the back of his head crashing. 'Alicia.' The name was beginning to mean something. 'Thanks for coming.'

'You look like shit.'

Nathan grinned, wiped the sleep from his eyes. 'You sweet talker.'

'How do you feel?'

'Like I look.'

'Ergh.' She touched the wire mesh that had been attached to his useless leg. He could feel the vibrations her fingers made, running right into his splintered bone. 'I'm sorry.'

'Sorry?'

'It's my fault, isn't it?'

'What do you mean?' Nathan looked at the needles jutting awkwardly in the veins of his wrists. Were they really necessary anymore? What in the name of God were they pumping into him?

'The saddle, the breast plate. It was no good. I should have noticed. I should have. . .' She trailed off, unable to find the words she needed.

Something she was saying didn't ring true. But what?

'I should have -'

Of course.

'Wait.' Nathan held up one hand.

'What is it?'

'I'm thinking.'

He had been talking to Christian. Christian was a security guard, or a bodyguard, or. . .

'Nathan?

He had been talking to Christian but he had been looking at Gertrude. Gertrude was being saddled up. Saddled up by. . .

'Nathan?'

'How could you have known?' he asked. 'You didn't saddle up the horse, did you?'

'But I checked it. It was my job to make sure it was okay.'

'When?'

'When what?'

'When did you check the saddle?'

'Just before you mounted. I checked it was all secure.'

'And you didn't notice any damage that might have caused it to break?'

'No.'

'No split, no weakness.'

'No, nothing.'

'And who actually put the saddle on the horse?'

'Nina.'

'The new girl?'

'Yes.'

'Strange. I saw who put the saddle on. It was someone I didn't recognise.'

'She is new.'

'It was a man.' Outside the window, the sun blazed hotly in a white sky. Bare trees stood by watchfully, naked, twisted boughs reaching up into splays of black wood. Interested birds hoped among the top parts of those trees, twitting and fluttering. Nathan watched with unfocussed eyes, his mind leaping from conclusion to conclusion. 'I saw,' he said. 'A young man.'

'There were no young men with us at Chepstow. I was with Gertrude, Nina was assisting the Governor, learning the ropes.'

'Why was Nina saddling up?'

'I. . .' Alicia looked down, flushed red.

'Alicia?'

'I had to see someone. It was important.'

Nathan slumped back into the pillows, head buzzing with possibilities. 'Who?' he asked.

'My boyfriend was there.' There was anger in her tone. Anger directed inwards, at herself. Nathan knew the sound of self-loathing well enough. His mother had spoken in that same tone for years.

'He wanted to talk to you about something?' Nathan asked.

Alicia nodded.

'So you left Gertrude?'

'No.' She looked up, green eyes gleaming. 'Nina was nearby. She knew what was going on and said she would look after the horse.'

'That was good of her.'

'I was only gone for a few minutes.'

'So was she.'

'So who saddled up?'

Nathan smiled distantly. 'Someone who wanted me dead.'

Chapter Fifteen

Nathan was sleeping again when Nina finally arrived at the ward, carrying a bunch of grapes, a stack of magazines and a net of oranges. She watched the jockey sleeping for a moment, leaned over, kissed his cheek. She read two of the magazines before he awoke.

'Man,' Nathan muttered groggily, 'all this lying around can really take it out of a guy.'

Darkness had descended on the outside world and Nina had already pulled the curtains closed. She was reading by the light of a standing lamp, angled in such a way that her face was impossible to distinguish in the gloom. In the corridor beyond the closed door, low voices discussed patients in the other wards. Plastic shoes squeaked on linoleum flooring. The smell of an uncertain death, a quiet loss, lingered in the air like sadness.

'Awake at last,' Nina said, putting the magazine to one side. 'I was beginning to think you just didn't like my company.' Her face remained in darkness. A prickle of uncertainty he could not explain ran across Nathan's shoulders.

'Nina,' he said. His voice was sharp and angular, almost painful to listen to. 'I was wondering when you were going to turn up. Lampar told me you've been around a lot this last week, keeping an eye on me.'

'Are you going to accuse me of waiting for an opportunity to smother you?' It was a joke, but there was genuine pain at its core.

'I wouldn't blame you if you were.'

Nina's shadow leaned forwards. Still no face. 'What's this? Self-pity?'

'I don't know.'

'I never thought you were the type.'

'You've sat with me through all this. After the things I've said, the things I've done. Why would you do that?'

She leaned back, plucked a grape from the bunch on the bedside table. There was a moment of contemplative silence. 'I'm not sure,' she said. 'It just seemed right. You looked so. . .'

'Lonely?'

'Dead.'

'Oh.'

'But worse somehow. Dead, but with nowhere to go, no-one to guide you.'

'You thought I needed your help?'

'I think you needed someone's. You looked like a man with no purpose, no reason to fight to stay alive. You were lost.'

'Is that why you were here? To guide me?'

A quiet laugh in the darkness. 'Maybe I was giving you a reason to come back. Something to latch on to in the real world.'

Nathan let the enormity of that simple gesture wash over him in a giant, gulping tide. She had wanted him to come back. She had wanted to be his beacon in the darkness, had wanted to hold his hand, even in death. She had wanted to guide him back, bind him to the world for which he cared so little. And he had never even phoned her. 'Christ. I've been such a bastard.'

'True enough. You've been the worst kind of bastard. But I don't think it's all been your fault. And you were right about one thing.'

'Which was?'

'I got this job to be closer to you.'

Nathan nodded. 'I suppose I owe you an apology of some description?'

'You owe me a whole bag full of apologies, but that can wait.'

'Until?'

'Until you take me out to dinner.'

Nathan grinned in the dark. 'Not waiting for me to take control any more, then?'

'I've done enough waiting in this hospital ward to last a lifetime.'

'Something's changed, hasn't it?'

'I think so, yes. I've changed. I suppose seeing you this way, lying there. Knowing that you'd. . . died. I thought I'd never see you again.'

'Why would you want to?'

'Because I don't believe you are the way you appear to be.'

'What does that mean?'

'It means I think you force yourself to be angry. I think you choose not to let anybody hurt you the way you've been hurt in the past. But secretly, somewhere inside you, there's a place that wants to open up again. I'd like to be the person it opens up for.'

'You think there's a better person in me?' His tone was self-deprecating.

'I know there is. You tried to bury him in years of hatred, but I can see him. I saw him when Neil tumbled at Aintree. I saw him when Mr Lampar killed himself. The man who wants to care.'

'And what if this hidden part of me opens up and there's only more darkness in there?'

'Then I'll be very surprised.'

There was a pause, eerie yet, somehow, comfortable. The silence was understanding.

'You're very special, aren't you?' Nathan said.

'Not to mention patient.'

'I wonder why I didn't see that early.'

'You never looked.'

'I suppose not, maybe you've opened my eyes.'

'Taken off the blinkers?'

'Something like that.' He sighed, allowed a moments peace to prevail while he judged how best to breach the subject of his accident with a girl who would most probably see his questions as accusations. 'I need to ask you something,' he said.

'Shoot.'

'Alicia told me you made up the saddle.'

Silence.

'Nina?' Nathan pressed.

'She told you that?'

'She had to go and meet her boyfriend. You were left in charge.'

'Yes, but I never saddled up.'

'Somebody did.'

'Alicia asked me to keep an eye on Gertrude while she sorted out some domestic problem with her boyfriend, that's true, but I was never asked to saddle up.'

'So who was?'

'I don't know.'

'You must have seen somebody with the saddle. You were there.'

'No, I was. . .' She stopped.

'No? You weren't there?'

Another silence, a longer pause. 'My father was at the course with some of his business associates. I only left the horse for a minute though.'

'You left the horse?' Nathan wanted to be angry, he should have been angry. Once he would have been furious, yet somehow he was not able to be. There was only a kind of resigned acceptance of the facts. Mistakes had been made, being angry couldn't make those mistakes different.

'I didn't even leave her,' Nina continued. 'I just turned my back. By the time I looked, she was already saddled and Alicia had returned. I just assumed she must have saddled up for you and I left her to it.'

'Alicia never put up that saddle, it was someone else, someone who wanted me to have a fall. Maybe somebody who wanted me dead.'

'You think. . ?'

'Yes, I think this may have something to do with my mystery postman.'

'Surely nobody would go to these lengths to see you take a spill?'

'Why not?'

'Who could be so cruel?'

'That's what I keep thinking about, and I keep coming up with the same answer. Neil.'

'Neil Jacobson?'

'It makes sense. He blames me for what happened at Aintree. He was brought on during my absence from Zypher Fields and he got comfortable, he wanted to take Tiff's runs so he orchestrated a little accident for me. I can't think of anyone else with such a motive.'

'It sounds sensible enough, but how can you prove any of it?'

'I can't.'

'So what are you going to do?'

'I don't know.'

'Maybe. . . Maybe this will all stop.'

'What makes you think that?'

'If this was all about rides, about being jocked off, it's all over. Neil got what he wanted, he's the first jockey now.' She laughed awkwardly, perhaps a little too optimistically. 'You're safe now.'

The door to the ward swung open suddenly and a sick, yellow light flooded into the room, cutting out the harsh outline of a female nurse and momentarily glancing across Nina's face before she had a chance to back further into the corner of shadow she had built up around herself. The nurse planted her feet firmly apart and thrust her hands on her hips.

'I'm going to have to ask you to leave, Miss,' the nurse said.

Nina remained concealed in the gloom, only the delicate line of her jaw being caught in the stray fingers of light that inched around the nurse's portly frame. 'Okay,' she said.

'Wait.' Nathan reached out and touched Nina's leg. 'Can we have five minutes, please, nurse?'

'Visiting hours are over.'

'Please?'

The nurse huffed, puffed, but Nathan was made of sterner stuff than straw and she relented ungraciously. 'Five minutes and I'll be back. Your lady friend will be gone by then.'

Nathan waited for the door to swing closed before he turned back to Nina. 'What happened to your face?' he asked.

'Sorry?'

'Your face. When the door opened, I saw.'

Nina appeared to shrink into the very corner of the room. 'Nothing. Just an accident in the stables yesterday.'

'What sort of accident?' Nathan forced himself to sit up.

'Nothing serious.'

'Lean forwards.'

'I. . .'

'Nina, lean forwards.'

There was a moment's hesitation, then she moved closer so that her face came into the light from the lamp. Her tiny eyes glimmered in large, round purple bruises, her bottom lip was hideously swollen. 'It looks a lot worse than it is,' she said.

'How did this happen, Nina?'

'I told you. It was a silly accident at the stables. I wasn't paying attention.'

'This was your father, wasn't it?'

'No.' Her tone was agitated.

'Nina?'

'It was my fault, okay?'

'How can you think that?'

'I'm too outspoken, I've got a big mouth. I should learn to keep quiet.'

'Nobody deserves to have this done to them.'

Nina moved back out of the light, concealing her face in blissful shadows, but that battered look would be forever imprinted in Nathan's memory. His anger - anger for the fate of another; anger he had before not even been aware he possessed - seethed uncontrollably.

Nina touched her cheek. 'He does it because he loves me.'

'Loves you? Look at yourself. You look worse than me and I was run over by a horse. How can you possibly say this is about love?'

Nina sprang up. 'And what would you even know about love?'

'Don't take this out on me.'

'Then don't start passing judgement on people you don't know.' She turned away, resting her hands on the windowsill where a gangly, ill-looking pot plant had been situated in order to 'brighten up the place'. Brightening up the place had obviously not extended to actually watering the plant. 'You aren't there,' Nina whispered. 'You don't see what it's like, what I do to make him so angry.'

'Whatever you do, it can't be deserving of this kind of treatment.'

'I'm bad sometimes.'

'You need to talk to someone about this. You need to get some help.'

Her hands clenched, her head bowed. An inner turmoil raged, unheard, unseen. 'Who do I talk to?' she whispered. 'Who can help me?'

'The police.'

'He's my father.'

'He's hurting you.'

'Sometimes people get hurt. That's just the way life is.'

'I don't understand you.'

'Maybe that's the problem.'

'Come over here. Sit down.'

She turned back, paced across the room. Her hands were solid by her sides, her back straight, breathing forced. She sat next to him on the bed, casting her face in silhouette against the lamplight. 'Can we talk about something else?' she asked.

Nathan touched her cheek carefully. 'Won't you tell me why he did it?'

'He's trying to protect me.'

'From something worse than this?'

'From you.'

'Why?'

'He. . . He knows about the party. After that night we. . .' She shook her head. 'I told him yesterday that I loved you. He doesn't understand how I could, after everything you did before.'

'So he hit you?'

'He wants me to be happy.'

Nathan fixed her with his gaze, shocked to feel a rogue tear welling in his eye. 'You faced that for me?' he asked.

'Is it so surprising?'

'I can't. . .'

She pressed a finger to his lips. 'Stop it,' she said. 'The worst is over now.' She leaned in, kissed him softly on the cheek. Her breath was warm, her hair fell forwards. His lips found hers. A multitude of horses, like a cliché in an old black and white movie, thundered in the silence of the ward.

Time. Inconceivable time.

The world unravelled.

But this wasn't right. This beautiful girl, this young and fantastic creature, had done something to him, had crawled into his dreams, had entered his mind even as he died. This girl had tried to get closer to him, had given everything to spend time around him. This girl had, in a way he could not explain, found a chink in the armour he did not even realise he wore. This most wonderful of all the angels had reached inside of him and found the human he had tried to bury in anger. This girl, whose trembling breath was now his own, had allowed her father to. . .

He pulled away, horrified.

'I can't do this,' he said, almost suffocated by the words. 'I can't let you do this.'

'Do what?'

'If this goes further, what does your father do next?'

'I'm not scared of him.'

'But I'm scared what he may do. If he realises we're together, what's he going to do to you?'

'I'm not going to live my life in fear.'

'And you shouldn't be expected to.'

'It will get better.'

'How?'

'It has to, things always do.'

'You have to inform the police.' Nathan drew a steady breath. Only now did he understand Corelli's misery. Only now did he understand how hard it was to try and do the right thing. 'We can't have a relationship if you don't,' he added, hopelessly.

There was a flash of anger in Nina's eyes. 'Are you asking me to choose?'

'If that's what it takes. I can't stand by and which this happen to you, and I refuse to be responsible for the way he treats you.'

'Isn't this my choice?'

'I don't think so.'

She stood. 'Always have to be in control, don't you?' she spat.

'This isn't about control. This is about reason. You can't let this happen.'

'He'll have to stop sooner or later.'

'When he kills you? When he. . ?' Nathan's eyes widened. 'When he kills me?'

'What are you saying?'

'I think you know what I'm saying. You said your father was there at Aintree. Why?'

'That's not your business.'

'He distracted you while you were looking after the horse. What was it he wanted?'

'He just needed to talk to me.'

'And that couldn't wait?'

'Ten minutes ago you were accusing Neil.'

'And you were all too eager to go along with that explanation, weren't you?'

Nina lashed out, striking Nathan across the cheek which only moments before she had kissed so tenderly. There were huge wells of tears spilling down her face. 'Bastard,' she hissed, before turning and running out into the yellow corridor. The squeak of her shoes on the linoleum receded into the distance.

Nathan slumped back in the pillows and closed his eyes. 'Shit,' he said.

The darkness pressed in.

Chapter Sixteen

She left.

The girl, whom Nathan had fallen in love with while he had been asleep and she had wrapped her soft arms around him, was gone. The girl to whom Nathan owed his very life had simply moved away.

She never even said goodbye.

Nathan took it much harder than he ever thought he would.

Apparently, her father had a flat in London and she had gone to spend a few weeks there before looking for a job further North. Nathan even thought about following her up there for a while.

He never did.

Instead, he focussed all his energy on recovering from the accident and, once all the various meshes and cages and splints came off, adjusting to life with a cane. It was, he would often say, 'a much more casual existence'. Sometimes he would be more honest and use the term 'dull'.

But Nathan's life had not been destined to be dull for long.

*

'Neil. So good to see you.'

Nathan answered the door wearing a smile that dutifully concealed the true nature of why he had invited Neil to visit the cottage.

'Nathan.' Neil's smile was more genuine, almost convincing, but Nathan was certain he detected the faintest glimmer of malice in the jockey's eyes. 'How are you getting on with the leg?'

Nathan ushered Neil through to the lounge and directed him to the most comfortable chair. 'I get a little nervous around magnets, I'll never be able to get a job as airport security, but apart from that I couldn't be better. Can I get you a drink?'

'Whiskey would be great.'

Nathan hobbled to the drinks cabinet, his cane clattering noisily. 'Ice?'

'Fine.'

Nathan splashed whiskey around two glasses and added crushed ice from a caddy. He balanced both glasses in one hand and supported his weight on his cane as he crossed the room. Neil watched with a barely concealed disquiet. 'Thanks,' he said, taking one of the glasses. 'You should sit down.'

Nathan gulped his whiskey. 'I'll stand,' he said. His fingers snaked around the brass ball of the cane. 'Leg gets stiff if I sit for too long.'

'Must be hard.'

'It's full of metal, it would be.'

'Still haven't lost the sense of humour, then?'

'Not quite yet, but there's still time.'

Neil frowned, sipped his whiskey. 'What are you going to do now?'

'You mean now I can't race? Or do you mean now that you've been taken on as a retained jockey and you get my house?'

Neil looked around nervously. 'Oh. You heard about that?'

'Of course I heard about it. I've been asked to move out as soon as I'm able.'

'You know, I don't need this cottage. I told Lampar that, but he insisted. Says the retained jockey has to take the house. He wants me around so he can keep an eye on me, but I could always find somewhere else.'

Nathan tapped his foot with his cane, spoke without looking at Neil. 'Don't be silly, Neil. This is what it's all been about, isn't it?'

'What all what's been about?'

'The letters, the saddle.' His knowing grin split into a terrible sneer. 'Even your fall at Aintree.'

'My fall?'

'I must admit, that was probably the most convincing part of the act. Risky too.'

Neil set down his glass with a shaking hand. 'I don't understand you.'

'I mean, who would risk serious injury just to make sure they didn't win a race? And you were so convincing with it.' The cane tapped rhythmically against his shoe, faster now. 'And to think I felt sorry for you. You certainly pulled the wool over my eyes. For a while, anyway.'

'You think I threw myself?'

'It makes sense.'

'Why would I do something like that? Why would I risk so much?'

'Because you knew about Corelli's problems. The poor guy was losing the plot for months and it wasn't any great secret. Even I knew about it, and I hadn't been speaking to him.'

'This is nonsense.' Neil rose as if to leave. Nathan's cane flashed angrily, in the sunlight streaming through the lounge window, jabbing against Neil's shoulder and forcing him back in his chair. Neil's look of confusion exploded into one of rage. 'I don't know what you think you're going to achieve, Nathan, but you are playing a dangerous game. Let me go.'

Nathan kept the cane pressed against Neil's shoulder, kept his smile bright and playful. 'You'd know all about dangerous games, wouldn't you?'

'You're crazy. I think that accident did more than smash your leg.'

'Really?' Nathan leaned forwards, exerting a little more pressure on the cane. 'If you really think that, you best stop playing dumb, because crazy people have a tendency not to be held accountable for their actions.' His eyes narrowed.

'Nathan, I haven't done anything to you. Whatever you might think. We're friends, we've been friends for years.'

'I don't suppose you ever thought Corelli would go so far as to kill himself, that couldn't have been part of the plan. But you knew he blamed me, and your loss would be just enough to push him over the edge, make him want to kill me. It's clever, I'll admit that. You get rid of me and you don't even get your hands dirty in the process. Cowardly, but clever.'

'Nathan.' Neil winced as the cane twisted, drilling into his shoulder painfully.

'Shut up.'

'Nathan, listen to yourself. This is a paranoid delusion.'

'Of course, Corelli was never meant to kill himself, but he did, and maybe you could use that to your advantage as well? Yes, why not? I take a few weeks out to clear my head and just look who's there to fill my shoes. Maybe you thought I would never come back, maybe you thought you would excel in my absence and just quietly edge me out of the equation.'

'I was helping Lampar. You left him at extremely short notice, I was available. There's nothing sinister about that.'

'Nothing sinister?' The cane flashed away from Neil's arm, dropping back to Nathan's side where it began to tap-tap-tap against his foot again. The sun glimmered through the window, spangling the walls with honey blossom patterns. Nathan's eyes were drawn to the half-full whiskey glass on the table. 'Aren't you going to finish your drink, Neil?' he asked.

'Pardon?'

'Your whiskey. That's my good stuff. It shouldn't go to waste.'

Neil rubbed his shoulder, his eyes full of doubt. 'You are cracked.'

Nathan looked down at his leg. 'No, not cracked.' The cane blurred into action, slamming down on the whiskey glass and shivering a powder of sparkles through the air. 'Shattered,' he roared. 'Not cracked, not broken. Shattered. My life is shattered.'

Neil covered his face as the last flecks of glass pinged off the coffee table. 'I'm sorry,' he screamed. 'I'm sorry about what happened, but it wasn't me.'

'You're the only one with a motive, Neil. You got too comfortable while I was away. When I came back you thought I was going to take back all the rides so you tried to scare me off with pathetic letters stuck on my car or on my door.'

'Letters?'

'Stop playing dumb,' Nathan screamed. The cane slashed down, slamming in the soft padding of the couch only millimetres from Neil's head. 'I know it was you, just admit it.'

'Nathan, what letters are you talking about?'

'Death threats. You were jealous of what I was capable of and you thought the notes would scare me off, send me packing back to Ireland.' Nathan paced nearer, a horrible, loping shuffle; the steps of a cripple. 'But I wouldn't go. I was too determined not to be afraid. So you organised for me to have a little accident. The proper adjustments were made to my saddle and the rest is history. And nobody would ever suspect you.'

'I wasn't even at Chepstow.'

'Keep talking, Neil.'

'You know I wasn't there. I didn't even have access to the horse you were riding that day. This, none of this, has anything to do with me.'

Nathan tightened his grip on the ball of the cane. His arm was trembling, his eyes dark, jaw set. 'If it wasn't you, tell me who it was.'

'I can't.' The fear was unconcealed in Neil's voice. 'I don't know anything.'

'You wanted my job.'

'Yes, of course I wanted your job. Why wouldn't I want your job?' He was crying pitifully, fat tears rolling down his cheeks. 'You were getting all the chances and I was getting all the scraps. But I wasn't the only one who wanted to be like you, to be you. You're one of the best, I mean, you were. I would have done anything to have all the breaks you had, but not this. Never this.'

Nathan stepped back, suddenly surveying the scene as if for the first time. His friend - his colleague - was sitting on the couch, crying hopelessly into his hands. Crying with fear, anger, hurt, embarrassment. Crying like a child.

'I would never hurt you. I would never take racing from you,' Neil said.

'Neil?' Nathan's eyes widened with terror. The cane thudded as it hit the rug by his feet. He had done this. He had reduced his friend to this terrible, pitiful, crying thing. In just a few minutes he had turned a proud man to a snivelling wreck.

He had done this.

'We were friends, Nathan. I would never begrudge you your success. You're better than me. You've always been better than me. I would never do anything like this. I wouldn't destroy your livelihood. I couldn't be that cruel to you.'

Nathan's mouth worked silently, his eyes huge with realisation.

'We were friends,' Neil sniffed.

'My God.' Nathan dropped into a seat, his hands flexing spastically. 'Jesus. What am I doing? Neil. I'm sorry, I'm so sorry.'

'Sorry?'

'I don't know what I'm doing anymore. Everything's so strange.'

'Nathan, what's going on?' Neil wiped his eyes. The sun glistened on shards of broken glass.

'I don't know. Somebody did this to me and I don't know why. Someone wanted to hurt me.'

'This sounds crazy.'

'Maybe it is. Maybe the fall has done something to my head, but I can't trust anybody, I can't even trust myself. I'm totally alone.'

'You don't have to be.'

'I've turned everyone away.'

'Then get outside help.'

'Maybe I should just commit myself to an asylum.' He strangled a sob in his throat, desperate to stay in control. 'How can I put things right between us now?'

Neil straightened up. 'Nathan, nobody can be expected to go through what you've been through these last few months without losing something on the way. It's understandable. You aren't yourself at the moment, you need to relax.'

'Relax?'

'Take some more time out. Get well. I'm sure this will all work out.'

'I wish I could be so certain.'

'What do you think they want, these people who are tormenting you?'

'Honestly? I don't know. Maybe they want me dead, maybe they just want me to stop racing.'

The letterbox rattled noisily. Nathan looked at Neil. Neil looked back.

'Expecting anything?' Neil asked.

'No.'

'Want me to go take a look?'

'If you would.'

Neil walked out into the hallway. When he came back he was holding a folded piece of white, square paper.

'Have you read it?' Nathan asked.

Neil's face was pale, drawn. He nodded.

'Fan mail?'

'Not exactly.'

'I guess whoever is doing this isn't happy with crippling me.'

'I agree,' Neil said. 'He won't be happy until you're dead.'

Chapter Seventeen

Outside help.

Neil's suggestion.

It couldn't hurt to get the opinion of somebody in the business of personal security, could it?

'Do you have all of the letters?' Christian Quigley asked, sitting at the kitchen table and purposefully folding his sunglasses before slipping them into the breast pocket of his immaculate suit.

Nathan leaned back against a worktop. The percolator hissed and spumed coffee into a glass jug. The other two suited men walked around with the same important air with which they had arrived, poking in cupboards, leaning out windows. Nathan couldn't quite tell whether they were working or simply being curious.

'Is it normal for three of you to turn up to a meeting like this?' Nathan asked.

Christian smiled, a wide, open smile that appeared as broad as his gigantic shoulders. Without the sunglasses he looked about as scary as Mickey Mouse. His eyes sparkled with an obviously playful nature and when he spoke it was not with a rumble but a calculated purr. 'Carl's a new boy to this,' he said, which, although not being an actual answer, seemed close enough for Nathan to accept it as such.

'Which one's Carl?' he asked.

'You think I can tell the difference?'

The two prowling associates straightened up in unison. They appeared to have been formed in the same mould and, while not twins, the suits they wore and the general presence of authority with which they conducted their not-entirely necessary search suggested they were part of the same breed.

The coffee percolator spluttered to silence; Nathan removed the jug.

'How does everybody want it?' he asked.

'Warm and wet,' Christian said.

'Sugar, cream,' Carl - or possibly not Carl - said.

'Black,' the other one said.

Nathan poured four cups of coffee. A moment of absorbed contemplation passed between the four men as they drank silently.

'The letters,' Christian said, eventually.

'I've got four of them,' Nathan said, pulling open a drawer and removing the offending articles. He dropped them on the table as though it burned his fingers to hold them. 'There were more, but I've been destroying them.'

'Destroying them?' Christian raised an eyebrow. The other two men - for surely they must have been men beneath the suits - tutted, almost inaudibly.

'When they first started I couldn't believe it was anything more than a sick joke. Later, I was too angry to keep them in the house so I used to burn them out back. Since the accident -'

'Accident?'

Nathan waved at his lame leg and then the cane resting against the wall nearby. 'I say accident, but I don't believe it was anything of the sort.'

'I read about it in the papers, Mr O'Donnell. It must be difficult not being able to do what you love.'

'It's rare in life anybody gets to do something they truly love.' A taste of coffee. 'People get by, though.'

'I'm sure. So, since the. . . incident, how many letters have you received?'

'Only these,' Nathan gestured at the letters spread on the kitchen table.

Christian picked up the closest note and read it thoughtfully. 'Do you remember what order these arrived in?'

'Is that important?'

'Possibly.'

Nathan leaned over and scanned each note. He hated even to look at them, to read those words of hatred, those strings of bile. All that thick, black type. Not the type he had wanted though. Not the black type used in an auction catalogue to prove his chosen steeds were the finest in Britain. All this type served to prove was somebody, somebody close, wanted him dead. Somebody despised him truly and it was almost painful to know it.

'That was the first,' he said, jabbing an accusing digit at one of the letters. 'That one came through the letterbox last Tuesday.'

'Through the letterbox?' Christian took the note and read it. *'I understand you. You are alone and you want everybody to feel the same. It isn't enough for you to suffer as they do. It isn't enough until you die. Just die.'*

'My biggest fan.'

'Interesting.'

'Interesting?'

'You say this came on Tuesday?'

Nathan lowered himself carefully into a chair and stretched out his leg with a groan of protest. It had been hurting more these last few days, a constant, niggling pain that wouldn't leave him alone. 'Tuesday afternoon,' he confirmed.

'That's four letters in less than a week. Have they always arrived this close together?'

'Only since the accident. Why? Is it important?'

'Possibly.'

'Not very forthcoming, are you?'

'Not often. Which was the second letter?'

'That one.' Nathan pointed out the note without touching it.

'Through the letterbox?'

'Yes. Is that impor. . ?' Nathan stopped, smiled. Christian smiled back.

'They always come through that way?'

'No. The first ones were on the car outside, then they were stuck to the front door. Only these ones have actually come through the letterbox.'

Christian nodded as though this was some great and terrible secret revealed after millions of years. He read the note. *'You pass through their lives, but they are trapped in yours. I will free them all. Die, Mr O'Donnell. Die and burn in Hell.'* Christian chuckled in a way that was not entirely to Nathan's liking. 'At least we know he's sending them to the right address.'

'A real weight off my mind,' Nathan said.

'Third one?'

Nathan pointed.

'It all ends in blood. What you have taken I cannot return, but I can take more from you. I will cut your heart, Mr O'Donnell. You will die, I will make certain of that. You will die.'

'Not very original, is he?' Nathan said.

'Persistent, I would say.'

The two nearly-nameless suits standing by the door looked at their watches in synchronisation and then looked out of the window as though they expected to see the postman come whistling down the driveway.

Christian took the last letter. 'This is the most recent delivery?'

'Impeccable logic.'

'Time is running out, Nathan. Death awaits you.'

'We've progressed to first name terms,' Nathan said wryly.

'It must be nice to be important.'

'Warms my heart.'

'And when did this note arrive?'

'Yesterday.'

Christian knitted his fingers together beneath his chin thoughtfully. 'I think, maybe, you contacted us just in time.'

'What makes you say that?'

'We'll get to that in a minute.' There was a pause for coffee. Nathan waited patiently. 'Tell me, have all the notes been written in this way?'

'What way?'

'Like these.'
'From newspaper cuttings?'
'No, the content. Have they all been phrased in the same way?'
Nathan's brow creased with puzzlement. 'They all suggest I should die a horrible and, as yet, undisclosed death. Is that what you mean?'
'Not exactly. These letters refer to other people, suggesting you have hurt them in some way. These letters all suggest that the author is seeking some kind of retribution for something you may or may not have actually done.'
'The first one just asked me to die. Later ones said something about the hurt I had inflicted and the emptiness in my soul.'
Christian nodded understandingly. 'That would tie in with what I'm seeing here. Tell me, has your name ever appeared in any of the notes, besides the ones you have here?'
'No. Why?'
'This is good coffee, by the way.'
'Thanks. What do you make of these letters? Am I in any danger?'
'Personally, I think you've seriously annoyed someone.'
'You think?'
Christian smiled that broad, open smile. 'Have you told the police about this?'
'No.'
'Why not?'
Nathan sighed and massaged his knee. It felt as though there were diamonds beneath his skin and as he kneaded them they exploded with miniature pain. 'You have to understand, I'm a celebrity. I didn't want a big thing being made out of this if it was only a silly prank. That's the kind of press I could do without considering everything that's been going on in my life recently.'
'I can understand that, but you may want to reconsider. This isn't a prank. I think you're in serious danger.'
'And the bad news?'
'You are an unusual man, Mr O'Donnell, but I like you. I'd like to

help you.'

'There's a first time for everything.'

'Okay, so, the next move is up to you. Do you want my help?'

'Do I get to know what I need helping from before I hand over the money?'

'Somebody out there wants to gut you like a fish. What else do you need to know?'

Nathan shrugged. 'Is a cheque acceptable?'

*

In the late afternoon, the two suits, Carl and - as it turned out - Marvin, went into the grounds to scout the area for possible access routes for a prowler and possible positions from which a sniper might be able to take a pot shot. That there was even the remotest possibility of a sniper taking cracks at him was impossible for Nathan to comprehend.

'Is this really as serious as you make it sound?' he asked.

Christian had moved through to the lounge and had already checked the locks on all the windows and doors. He was now relaxing in Nathan's most comfortable chair. 'I think so, yes,' he said.

'But why? It's just a few letters.'

'And what about your little incident at Chepstow?'

'Could be coincidence.'

'Could be, but the notes say it isn't enough for you to suffer. I think your fall was organised to either kill you or cause you as much pain as possible before you died. Probably the latter.'

Nathan eased his way over to the drinks cabinet and fixed himself a hefty shot of whiskey. 'You think the notes and the accident are related then?'

'I'd stake money on it.'

'But why would somebody want me to suffer? If they want me dead, fine. But to try and destroy me first? Why would anyone do that?'

'You'd have a better idea than me, but I think you did something, probably without realising,' - a faint, knowing smile - 'that hurt somebody. My guess would be it hurt them a lot. Now they want to hurt you back.'

'They couldn't have known that the fall would stop me racing though.'

'Maybe they got lucky.'

Nathan glugged his whiskey in a single swallow and fixed himself an even larger measure. 'You're that certain the two things are linked?'

'That's why the notes have changed.'

'Changed?'

'Your stalker is working in phases. Phase one was simply to upset you, to cause you disquiet. The note was short and brutal. Shocking. The fact there was no motive described, no reason, would only make it seem more appalling and cause it to play on your mind. Your friend didn't want it to appear like a prank, he didn't want you to dismiss it.'

'I suppose that makes sense.'

'Once he'd got your attention it was simply a matter of dropping the occasional note on your car to let you know that he hadn't forgotten. You have some sleepless nights, you start to suspect everybody. You push away the people who care about you, completely isolate yourself. Bingo. You are alone, vulnerable.

'Phase two was to make you suffer. He organised a little fall for you, took away your career, your ambition, even your home.'

'You keep saying 'he'. You think this is a man?'

'Possibly.'

'I knew you were going to say that.' Nathan moved across to the couch and sat. His leg throbbed but the whiskey was helping.

'So he ruins your life, because he thinks you deserve to endure the ruin and hurt he has endured at your hands. Phase two is complete.'

'And what's phase three?'

'He kills you.'

'For a minute, I thought you were going to say something cheerful.'

'You must realise, you are dealing with a seriously disturbed individual here. He's getting closer to you and he wants you to know it. The places where the notes are left are more important than you think. They were placed on the car first, somewhere outside. Then he stuck them on the front door. Now he's pushing them through the letterbox, actually putting them in the house.' Christian smiled coldly. 'He's moved from outside the house to inside in just a few days. He's got closer.'

Nathan drained his whiskey glass. 'I never even thought,' he said.

'The letters too. First he didn't use names, then it was Mr O'Donnell. Now, it's Nathan. It's like he thinks he knows you, he's closer.'

'But what does that mean?'

'It means that within the next few days, your stalker will make an attempt on your life.'

Nathan slumped back in the couch and closed his eyes. This couldn't be happening. This was crazy. 'What do I do?' he asked.

'The first thing you have to do is believe this is real. I know what you're thinking. You're thinking it's all too ludicrous, like something in a movie. But this is real life and the risks are real.'

'I don't even know what I'm supposed to have done.'

'Maybe you should start thinking about it. Do you have any ideas who might be sending you these letters?'

'Don't you?'

'I know what I think.'

'Which is?'

Christian arranged himself more comfortably in his chair. 'I think it's someone who you didn't know before all of this started, but now it's someone close to you. Who have you got on your list of possibles?'

'List?'

'Come on, you must have a list. You can't possibly not have pondered who is doing this to you. Run them off. Give me some names.'

Nathan shook his head. 'I don't know. I've gone through all the people who might have been responsible and ruled them out for one reason or another. I can't think of anyone else.'

'Try me. Go through the ones you ruled out.'

Nathan dredged up all the names that had bounced around his head for the past few months. The room appeared to grow darker. Rain lashed against the windows, leaving sticky rivulets of spittle on the glass. 'Okay,' he said. 'There was Lady Cavanaugh.'

'This isn't a woman. I'm almost certain of that.'

'Really?'

'There's a lot of violent pride in those letters. Man's vanity.'

'Then I guess that rules out Nina as well.'

'Nina?'

'She used to work here. I thought, for a while, she might be the one responsible for this.'

'Why did you suspect her?'

'I don't know.' Nathan sighed and drummed his fingers against the side of his empty whiskey glass. 'Because I'm a fool.' He paused. 'She wasn't like anyone else I've ever met. She was beautiful and she really cared. I treated her badly, worse than she deserved, and she still loved me.' He blinked the unexpected tears from his eyes. Did not look at Christian. 'I let her go. She wanted to be with me and I wouldn't let her.'

'Why not?'

'I wouldn't let her get too close, I couldn't allow that to happen. I hurt her again. Even after I knew how much she cared.'

Christian watched silently.

'Why would I hurt her again when I knew how she felt for me?'

'Maybe you couldn't help it. . . Did she ever say why she loved you so much?'

'No.'

'She never said anything?'

'She was special. I think she wanted to save me.'

'Do you need saving?'

'I shouldn't have let her go.'

Christian laughed, a short, harsh laugh that snapped Nathan's head up. 'Women, who needs them? Come on, give me some more names.'

Nathan composed himself admirably. 'Lord Cavanaugh.'

'Why?'

'Because I was sleeping with his wife.'

'You and a hundred others, I shouldn't doubt. Cavanaugh's too old to care, certainly too old to worry about organising death threats. If he treats his wife like a possession, dragging her around draped in diamonds, then what does he expect? He's never treated her the way she deserves. And his son, before you say it, can't even tie his shoelaces, let alone make this kind of violent threat.'

Nathan lowered his sad eyes. 'There was Neil. My friend.'

'A jockey?'

'Yes.'

'Certainly not him. Like I said, this is somebody you only met recently. Besides, no jockey would do something so awful to a colleague.'

'I know.'

'Anybody else on your list?'

'Everybody's been on my list at some point. My Governor, all the stable hands, all the connections for every horse I've ever ridden, and ever refused to ride. Even Corelli, before he. . .' He trailed off hopelessly. 'Even Corelli's wife.'

'Is there anybody who actually likes you?' Christian asked.

'Mum loved me.'

The rain hammered at the window, seeking admittance with its persistent, stabbing fingers. Christian cleared his throat. 'Have you ever thought. . . Maybe this isn't to do with you.'

'What do you mean?'

'Now, tell me if I'm wrong, or if I'm overstepping the mark, but I heard your father was. . .'

'Oh.' Nathan physically recoiled at the idea. 'No. It couldn't be that. My father died a long time ago and I never knew about the things he did in Ireland until after my mother passed away.'

'That doesn't mean you should rule it out as a possible explanation.'

'Nobody could hold me responsible for those things. I can't believe that.'

'But then, you still find it hard to believe anybody wants you dead at all.'

Nathan pushed himself out of his chair and hobbled across to the window. Darkness lay heavy upon the world, shadowing the movements of the night creatures. Only the narrowest sliver of the moon attempted to illuminate a world of sinister shapes. There were no stars. 'Where are your colleagues?' Nathan asked.

'They're very thorough. They won't come back to the house tonight.'

'The night came in fast.'

Christian rose and stood alongside Nathan, resting a hand on his shoulder. 'The darkness is never far away. I suggest you move away from the window.'

'Move away?'

'We have to assume the worst of your stalker. He's obsessed enough to bring notes to your house, so he will want to make the hit himself, to see your face before you die. Standing in front of the window gives him the perfect opportunity.'

Nathan backed away, pressing his back to the wall. 'Surely you can't believe this person is going to shoot me in my own home?'

'This isn't your home anymore. He made sure of that.' Christian's open, beaming smile masked the seriousness in his voice. 'I doubt he intends for you to die that way, though. He will want to be close when it happens. Maybe he'll even make like he wants to shake hands with you, or get an autograph. Whatever he does, you will see your killer's eyes before the end.'

'You really are a ray of sunshine.'

'You're not paying me to sugar-coat what's happening here, Mr O'Donnell. From now on, myself or one of my associates will be with you at all times, for the duration of our contract.'

'And if the killer makes his move?'

'We move faster.'

Nathan bowed his head, leaned heavily on his cane. 'So that's it? We wait?'

'We can take steps to ensure your safety, but we aren't investigators. If you want this stalker caught, you will need to speak to the police.'

'I suppose, after everything you've told me, I wouldn't feel so awkward doing that, but they're hardly going to put a lot of effort into an investigation based around a few notes. They won't do anything until somebody has made some gesture of violence towards me.'

'So, until then, we'll make sure you're ready for any eventuality.'

Nathan limped across to the drinks cabinet and shook whiskey into his glass. 'Drink?' he asked.

'Best not for now. I'm going to make a tour of the house, check for any breaches in security.'

Nathan watched as Christian moved out into the hallway. 'Breaches in security? Jesus, this used to be my home. When did it become a prison?' The mellow fire of whiskey burned through his stomach. Closed his eyes.

Listened.

Christian's footsteps on the stairs.

The moaning of the wind around the eaves; the cottage creaking and settling.

The drumming of the rain.

Christian's footsteps in the upstairs hallway.

His own heartbeat, the rush of blood in his ears; the almost audible throb of pain in his crippled leg. His shallow breathing.

Christian's footsteps in the master bedroom.

Nathan fumbled a packet of unopened cigarettes from his trouser pocket and ripped off the foil. He found his lighter in the other pocket and struck up a flame. Hot smoke flushed through his lungs in a calming wave. More whiskey splashed into his glass.

Christian's footsteps thumped out of the bedroom and into the spare room.

The front doorbell rang.

The front doorbell. . .

Nathan looked up, a hard rod of fear straightening his back. The cigarette dropped from his mouth and into the whiskey glass where it hissed aggressively. 'Christian?' he called.

Christian's footsteps padded to the top of the stairs. 'What are you doing?' he called down.

'Did you say your colleagues wouldn't be back tonight?'

The doorbell rang again.

Nathan glanced across at the dark window, the rain coursing over its smooth surface. Nobody from the manor would come down to the cottage in this weather. But there was a face at the window, just the same.

Nathan's breath choked.

'Get down,' Christian screamed. 'Nathan, get down.'

Running on the stairs.

A flash of motion outside the window.

Nathan threw himself on the floor, his hands wrapping over his head.

Christian appeared in the doorway, panic drawn in the lines of his face. 'Stay down,' he said, looking at the window. Nothing there. 'Somebody's moving around the house, looking for a way in.'

Nathan squeezed his eyes shut. This couldn't be happening. This wasn't real.

Christian ran to the front door and threw it open. Nothing there. The darkness of night stretched on into the heart of the storm. Nothing there.

Chapter Eighteen

'Go away?' Nathan asked, as he stood on the front porch in the cold light of morning, smoking the last cigarette from the pack he had opened the previous evening.

Christian paced agitatedly, his muscular bulk carried nimbly on sure feet, his hands wedged into the corners of his trouser pockets. His breath plumed when he spoke, his words freezing in the air. 'This is bigger than I thought,' he said.

'Bigger how?'

'I was upstairs in the spare room and I saw someone on the grounds. Not one of mine. You were in the lounge and you say you saw a face at the window. We both heard the doorbell ringing. That's three people. We aren't dealing with an individual here.'

Nathan dropped his cigarette and crushed it with the heel of his shoe. 'But you said -'

'I know what I said, but I was working under the impression that it was an individual. What we have here is a team of people working together, hence their ability to organise the incident at Chepstow.'

Nathan shook his head in disbelief. 'This can't be possible. One unbalanced individual with an absurd grudge I could understand, but not this.'

Christian's pacing quickened, his feet crunching in the damp gravel. 'It certainly puts a new spin on things. I can't believe all these people are delusional, and that means their grievance with you must have some kind of solid grounding.'

'I'm sorry?'

'For three people to believe you have done them wrong in some way would indicate that you probably have. It means we aren't dealing with psychologically disturbed individuals, we are dealing with normal, everyday people.'

'How can you say this is normal?'

'Perhaps not normal, but these people are going to be organised, well-prepared. There won't be anything random about their activities. That means you are in a lot more trouble than I thought.'

'So I should just leave?'

'For a few days. We need some time to re-evaluate the situation, to calculate a new course of action.'

'This is my home.'

'No, it isn't. This is just a place you're living in at the moment.' Christian sighed heavily, stopped pacing, fixed Nathan with a steel gaze that had none of the playfulness about it that he had exhibited the day before. 'Do you have any idea what happened last night? Do you know how unusual it is for a person to be targeted in this way? This isn't an everyday situation.'

'You deal with this sort of thing all the time.'

'Not like this. If those people had wanted you dead last night, I wouldn't have been able to stop them. You aren't dead, because they chose not to kill you. Tonight, maybe they won't go away. Maybe they'll keep going around the house until they find a way in.'

Nathan crossed his arms over his chest. 'What could I have done to them?' he asked.

'I think, perhaps, it might be time to start thinking about the people your father may have harmed before his death.'

'My father?'

'These people are organised, Mr O'Donnell, exceptionally so. They are probably watching us both right now. Your father was very. . . patriotic. He may have done things you know nothing about.'

'They can't hold me responsible for his actions. I didn't even know, How could I have known? This isn't fair.' Nathan's lips parted in an angry, scared snarl. 'Why should this happen to me? I'm not a politician? I'm not even a jockey anymore.'

'Some people cannot be reasoned with, Mr O'Donnell. Do you have somewhere we can go?'

'We?' Nathan's eyes narrowed into red slits of fire. 'We? You and your associates? How can I trust you?' He took a faltering step, hand tightening on his cane. 'You say these people are organised, well, you're organised. There are three of you. I barely even know you and you expect me to trust you?'

'I don't think you have any other option but to trust me.'

'I only have your word that there was someone out in the grounds when you were in the spare room. And where did your colleagues go? Why didn't they come back all night?' The accusations were hissed through clenched teeth.

Christian walked nearer with a quiet purpose. 'Mr O'Donnell,' he said, in that low, animal purr. 'I have a very good reason for wanting to keep you alive. You're paying my wages.' He put a hand on Nathan's shoulder and squeezed. 'Besides, if I wanted to kill you, I've had more than enough opportunities.'

'Okay. Fine. Tell me what I have to do.'

'Get away. Five days, a week, just long enough for us to get a better understanding of who might be doing this and, just as importantly, why.'

'A better understanding?'

'Marvin will stay behind at the cottage, make it appear like you're still living there.'

'Isn't that dangerous?'

'That's why you pay us so much. Meanwhile, Carl and myself will accompany you. If your stalkers follow us, then we will have a better knowledge of what we are dealing with. If they stay behind and move in on Marvin, he may be able to ascertain who the culprits are.'

'Follow us?'

'It's a possibility. If they have a directional microphone they may be able to pick up our conversations, that's why I don't want you to tell us where we're going. Organise it today, as soon as possible.' Christian smiled boyishly. 'And one small suggestion. Don't organise a trip to Ireland.'

'I have nowhere else.'

'Then think of somewhere.'

'But. . .' Nathan trailed off. There was somewhere. Somewhere he might still be wanted. 'Give me half an hour. I need to speak to my Governor.'

*

'Nina?'

Lampar sat at the head of the dining table, hands splayed on either side of a steaming cup of coffee. Various unnamed and oddly recognisable maids moved around the room, dusting and cleaning and occasionally trying to catch Nathan's eye. Nathan kept his gaze focussed in the bottom of his coffee cup. Now was certainly not the time to be renewing old acquaintances.

'Yes,' he said, and the word sounded sad and distant as it attempted to span the void between jockey and trainer.

Lampar looked at his watch. Ten o'clock and the mist had finally been driven from the gallops. 'You are aware,' he grumbled, 'Tiff' is running today.'

'I know, Governor.'

'I really haven't got time to waste in silly games.'

'I'm aware of that Governor, I did use to have something to do with this profession at one time and I appreciate your situation.'

Lampar frowned and a look of sadness passed across his face for an instant. 'Of course, sorry. I think I'm just a little tense. Neil will never be the rider you were.'

Nathan glanced out of the window across the stables. The land, with its myriad paths and boundaries, meandered lazily down the hill until it was rudely crossed by the black line of the snaking road. In just a short time Nathan would drive out on that road. Perhaps he would never return here.

The morning was crisp, new. White clouds, brittle and flaking around the edges, stretched across the pale sky and hid the half-lidded eye of the sun. Nathan saw the beauty of the world and the empty longing inside himself expanded horribly. Never before, not even after the death of his mother, had he felt so terribly alone.

He blinked tears from his eyes and wiped his cheeks before any of the maids could notice.

'Neil's a good jockey,' Nathan said, without diverting his gaze from the window. 'Think he may have to struggle against the going after the night we had, but he's got a good chance.'

'You truly believe that?'

'I'm glad he's going to be staying on here. He's never had too many breaks. I think he needs this one.'

Lampar drummed his fingers on the table, sucked his teeth thoughtfully. 'This doesn't sound like you, Nathan. What's wrong?'

Seagulls, a mess of white wings and snapping beaks, flocked in the distance, spinning and twirling playfully across the horizon. 'I don't know,' Nathan said. 'Looks like the storm's moved out to sea.'

'Nathan?'

Nathan blinked. 'I have to go away, Governor. I'll be moving out of the cottage a little sooner than I'd intended.'

'You don't need to do that. Neil's already said you take as long as you need.'

Nathan laughed and the sound came out as a protracted sneer. 'I'm out of time. Something I didn't even know was there has caught up with me. I have to move today.'

'Today?'

The seagulls bobbed and weaved hypnotically. 'I think, I've gone through my entire life without seeing things. Not the important things. I've realised that too late and I don't have time to put everything right.'

'So you're leaving?'

'I'm not sure I was ever really here.'

Lampar leaned forwards, his face a mask of puzzlement. 'Nathan, dear boy, what are you saying?'

'You never know you're on a peak until you're coming down, Governor. I never realised how much emptiness was in my life until someone made me see, and now there's nothing I can do.'

'I was hoping you'd stay on for me, as an assistant manager.'

Nathan laughed with a bitterness that stung the air. 'This isn't about work. I could have had something great, something I never even realised I wanted. I gave it all up needlessly.'

'Is this about Nina?'

The seagulls scattered, vanishing in the white sky. 'I need to ask you a favour,' Nathan said.

'Ask.'

'Don't move Neil into the cottage straight away. I have a. . . friend, who I would like to stay there for a few days.'

'What sort of friend?'

'I can't say, just please don't let Neil move in until I've contacted you.'

'Not a problem.'

Nathan paused. God, he was tired. Impossibly tired. 'I need something else.'

'Nina's address?'

'Am I that transparent?'

'You are.'

'Can you help me?'

Lampar clasped his hands together. 'You're not coming back, are you?'

Nathan closed his eyes and thought about that face at the window. Cold, dark, expressionless. Waiting in the dark for one single, clean shot.

'I won't be coming back,' he said.

Chapter Nineteen

'Just the Gazette, is it, Boss?'

Nathan drew his eyes back from an uncomfortable survey of the crowding faces moving around the train station. The face at his window last night had been almost indistinguishable in the gloom. It could have been anyone. Anyone here. 'Thanks,' he muttered.

'That's fifty pence then, Boss.'

Nathan snatched the paper away from the kiosk salesman. 'Keep the change.'

Beards, moustaches, glasses, wrinkles, lipstick, rouge, smiles, frowns. The faces travelled up and down the train station platforms. It could have been anyone.

Christian and Carl, in black suits and designer sunglasses, watched from a nearby bench. Nathan did his very best to act like he didn't know they were there.

In the Gazette, page thirty-three: Today's prices.

Nathan winced as he turned back to the kiosk, his lame knee throbbing violently. The salesman was watching him thoughtfully.

'You know who I am, don't you?' Nathan asked.

The salesman leaned forwards, a low animal cunning glimmering in vindictive eyes. 'Must be difficult, watching someone else ride her, Mr O'Donnell.'

Nathan glanced over his shoulder at the bench. Christian had disappeared. 'There'll be other races,' he lied. 'Thanks again.'

'Any chance of a signa. . .'

Nathan's brass-topped cane clattered on the platform as he hobbled away awkwardly.

Over the speakers, another announcement was made. A tinny, less-than-apologetic confirmation the train would still be some time in arriving.

Nathan sat, with a sigh, on the bench next to Carl, gratefully accepting a paper cup that was thrust unceremoniously in his face. 'This isn't decaffeinated, is it?' he asked.

No answer.

Nathan sampled the coffee. 'Any sign of them yet?' he asked.

Them. His would-be assassins.

No names. No faces.

Just Them.

Carl shook his head.

Several moments made an awkward but less-then-hasty retreat.

'Nothing unusual at all?' Nathan pressed.

'No.'

Nathan tried on a smile, turned his attention back to the paper.

Maybe it would be okay. Maybe he had more time than he realised. Maybe one wild night was all these people had ever wanted.

Maybe, just maybe. . .

He flicked through the pages of the Gazette.

The shadow fell across him.

*

Christian had been right. Nathan saw the eyes of his killer before he died.

But more horrible than seeing those eyes, more horrible than realising he was about to die, was the horrifying fact he didn't know why.

For all the terrible things Nathan had done in his life, for all the shameful, hurtful things, he had never once offended this towering man before him. For all the reasons he could have died, this was the one that was so totally and incomprehensibly devastating.

He saw the silenced muzzle of the nine-millimetre handgun level at his chest.

His mouth worked stupidly around idiotic syllables. What did I do? You have to tell me, what did I do?

You can't just shoot me, not without letting me know. I have to know.

What did I do?

What?

'I don't even have a mobile phone anymore,' he said

*

Death was a lot quieter than he had imagined it might be.

Before - before the gun went off - there had been a million sounds, a million voices, all combining in a roaring crescendo so familiar to the everyday man that it was barely even perceptible. But afterwards. . . Afterwards there was nothing, and the sudden absence of all those familiar, screaming, painful non-distractions was perhaps more terrifying to Nathan than the realisation he had been shot in the chest.

The rustle of the paper as he flicked through the story about street crime and mobile phones, the squeal and hiss of trains on the next platform, people talking on phones, even Carl breathing beside him. It had all been there, each sound layered on the next and becoming, ultimately, impossibly smudged.

Then the sound of footsteps approaching.

The ridiculous words coming out of his mouth. 'I don't even have a mobile phone anymore.'

The gun flaring, with a quiet whump, into fire and pain. Even his own strangled cry.

Then silence.

Nathan hit the floor and a defeated, resolute smile pushed the edges of his blood-choked mouth. After so much uncertainty, after so many years of lies, he finally knew something. Death was silent, and in the end, no matter who you were, you faced that silence alone. And in being alone, in experiencing your unique and once-in-a-lifetime-never-to-be-repeated death, you were sharing the experience of the billions of people who had been there before you and the billions who would come after.

So perhaps, for at least that one fleeting moment before never-ending darkness, Nathan did not feel alone anymore.

He only wished. . .

He only wished he could have seen her face one last time.

He only wished. . .

And on the very brink of the precipice, a shining thought erupted in his mind. At least he had sent the letter. . .

At least he had let Nina know. . .

The rest would be up to her.

Then afterwards - after the second shot had been fired and Nathan's life staggered, with one last bloody rattle in his throat, to its anti-climactic and desperately lonely conclusion - the rest of the world started to react.

Carl blinked, rose from the bench and took a single step nearer to the fresh corpse and the man crouched beside it. He tried to speak. For what seemed like hours the words stuck in the back of his throat and his mouth formed empty sounds. 'You,' he managed, and the assassin looked up triumphantly. 'You said you weren't going to do it. You said it was just to scare him.'

Christian straightened up, the gun still held in his shaking hand. 'You knew this was the aim. Don't pretend otherwise.'

Other people on the platform, those that had heard Nathan's cry and those that had since seen the corpse and the smoking gun in Christian's hand, were backing away. Hands were pressed to white faces, some people were running, two men vomited violently.

'Jesus.'

'Oh my God.'

'He shot him.'

'Somebody phone the police.'

'Somebody call an ambulance.'

'He's still armed.'

'Christ.'

'He's killed him.'

A widening circle was forming around the two suited men and the body lying between them. The brakes of the delayed train screeched as it finally pulled into the station, shuddering to a hopeful stop.

Christian fixed Carl with a stare that was truly insane. The crowd continued to jostle and move away. Some people were screaming now. Children were crying. The pool of blood issuing from Nathan's body was expanding and branching off in sickening, inquisitive fingers. Carl took a step backwards.

'What have you done, Christian?'

'I've finished it.'

'Finished what?'

'Finished what he started when he slept with my daughter.'

Carl's vision blurred with terrified tears. His gaze locked on the barrel of the handgun. 'You said he needed to be taught a lesson. You said he deserved what happened at Chepstow and I believed you. But how could he deserve this? What did he do?'

'He made her pregnant.' Christian spat the words like a curse. 'He slept with her, made her pregnant, then never even had the decency to contact her again.'

'I don't understand.'

'You don't have children, do you?'

'No.'

'Of course you don't, you're too young. You wouldn't understand.'

Several uniforms began to emerge through the crowd, police officers attempting to hold back the throng of people who were too scared to get any closer to the scene of the crime, but too interested to leave entirely. More shouting, more screaming, more crying. All those layers of sound. All smudged.

'Why here?' Carl said. 'You could have done this last night at the house.'

'I know.'

'Why do it here in front of these people? These people didn't need to see this.'

A violent, blood-lusty grin cut raggedly across Christian's face. 'I did it for them.' He waved at the pushing, pulling, never-constant crowd beyond the struggling police officers. 'I wanted them to see this. See this creature put down.'

'Why?'

'This man was supposed to be a hero, a great jockey. I want people to know what he was really like. I don't want him to be remembered as anything other than a pathetic, wasted cripple.'

'But all this?' Carl gestured wildly. 'All this just to ruin a man's reputation before you killed him? You're going to go to prison, Christian.'

Christian looked at the corpse, at the upturned, white eyes, the frozen grimace. 'You never had to sit up at night listening to your only daughter crying into her pillow because of something a monster like this had done to her.'

'Monster? Look at yourself, Christian.'

'I only did what any father would have done.'

'How can you believe that?'

'She was just a kid.'

Carl took a deep breath, swallowed hard, took a step towards Christian with his hands raised. 'Christian, what did you do?'

'I had to protect my daughter.'

'Your daughter isn't pregnant though, is she?' Another step closer.

'She used to be such a good girl. Never did anything to bring shame on the family. Then she met him and all this happened.' Christian sank to his knees next to the body that had, only moments before, been alive. Fragile, broken, but alive. 'I never want to hurt her but sometimes it's all she understands.'

More uniforms began to appear at the edge of the circle of gawping bystanders. A lot of the screaming and shouting had died down, an almost unnatural calm descended on the train station. The officers glanced nervously at each other.

'What did you do to her, Christian?' Carl said, risking another step.

'She couldn't keep the baby. I wouldn't let her keep the baby.'

'You made her have an abortion?'

Christian looked up and there was an unreasoning madness in his countenance. 'I wouldn't have had to make her do anything if it wasn't for this bastard.' He punched the corpse. The corpse jittered and for one horrible moment Carl was certain there was still life in the shattered rag doll. 'He treated her badly. He even told me. We sat in his lounge and I had to listen to him go on about how badly he had treated her. The man's an animal.'

'Look at yourself, Christian. You're covered in the man's blood.'

Christian looked at his gloved hands, then out at the crowd. A second ring of bodies had formed protectively in front of the first; a tighter circle of police helmets and jackets.

'Look what you've done,' Carl said. 'Just put down the gun and let this be over.'

'If I give myself up, you come with me. And Marvin. You both helped me organise this.'

'I'm walking away now, Christian. I'm going to turn myself in to one of these nice police officers. I would suggest you do the same.'

'You can't.'

'Watch me.'

Christian grinned maniacally. 'You saddled up the horse, Carl.'

Carl nodded and turned away. 'I can live with that. I hope you can.'

'Carl.'

'What?'

'I only did this for her.'

Carl looked back, saw Christian drop the gun and put his hands behind his head. At an unspoken command, several officers broke from the circle and quickly moved in to secure the area. 'I know you did,' Carl said, as Christian was wrestled, unresisting, to the ground. 'I just hope she sees it that way.'

Two police officers approached Carl, one casually jangling a set of handcuffs. Carl ignored them both, unable to tear his gaze from Christian being roughly dragged to his feet. There was nothing in Christian's coldly calculated eyes; a terrifying lack of any kind of remorse.

'You know that man?' the youngest of the two officers asked.

Those eyes. . .
'No.' Carl shook his head sadly. 'I don't think so.'

Chapter Twenty

Christian clasped his fingers together on the table as the guarded door opened and a stream of nervous-looking people wearing red 'visitor' vests shuffled inside. One by one they located the table where their husband or uncle or father or son was sitting. His fingers tightened as each face that appeared through the door was revealed to be someone he had never seen before.

God, let her come.

An old grey-haired woman hobbled in, a blank-faced guard assisting her to the table in the far corner where a young lad waited, casually slumped in his chair with a look that suggested he had been in a prison before and would more than likely be in one again at some point in the future. The woman eased into a chair and Christian was almost certain he could hear her bones creak. Perhaps all that creaked were the strained family ties that kept the old dear coming back.

Next, a family. Mother with two kids; a boy and a girl. Both too young to understand the terribleness of this uncompromising prison.

The mother looked good enough to be deserving of a wolf-whistle, if Christian had seen her on the outside, but under the circumstances he decided against it.

Please God, she had to come.

Please.

The two kids with the attractive mother recognised the unshaven forty-something loser at the back of the visitor centre as their father and dashed off to throw their arms around him. Christian had spoken with that man on several occasions; his name was Harold. He robbed banks for a living which, while not being totally original, must have been interesting work. He hugged his kids and cried in huge, wracking sobs that made some people on nearby tables slightly nervous. Christian squirmed awkwardly. He understood the father's pain and wondered why such a man would risk losing so much to knock over a bank. But why had Christian risked so much himself? Even his revenge had lost its significance within those hideous, damp walls, where the hollow nights were only interrupted by the crying of the lost and the jangle of the warden's keys.

Harold's wife was cooler in her approach and it was obvious she was only here through some sense of duty. It was almost a certainty that she was now sleeping with the manager of one of the banks her husband had raided, and who could blame her? She was attractive and she had married a fool.

Christian closed his eyes and tried to tell himself he was not such a fool as these other poor souls. When he could not convince himself, he returned to prayer, to the mantra by which he now lived: God, please let her come.

She had to come. He sent her the visitor's pass over a week ago.

Third up - third victim through the heavy-set and cruelly barred door - was a teenage girl. It had to be. . . but it wasn't his daughter. This girl had red hair and she was by no means as attractive. She looked around with strange, round eyes that made her look like a character from a Japanese cartoon. Those eyes finally fell on a young, handsome man in the middle of the room. The man was quite striking and in another time or place could have been a fashion model. He was clearly in love with the girl who had walked in but he remained dignified, only lightly touching her hand, as she sat down, to show his affection. Christian knew instinctively that this girl would be loyal to her boyfriend while he was inside.

He hoped they would make it.

Next through the door was an ageing man with white, feathery hair and glasses. He walked slowly, with an air of prolonged sadness through years of loneliness. He sat opposite a much younger man who clasped the elder's hand but said nothing by way of a greeting. Perhaps because to try speaking would cause both men to break down uncontrollably. The father-son relationship was a powerful thing, but not the same as the father-daughter bond.

And there she was. Suddenly, and just when he was beginning to lose hope. His beautiful, wonderful daughter.

Nina.

She sat. His hand moved across the table to touch hers and she retracted. Her mouth was a pale line, her eyes large and wet.

'Honey,' Christian said.

'Father,' she said.

'It's so good to see you. How have you been?'

Her dead eyes swivelled to focus on him. They were almost black in this poor lighting. 'I've been better,' she said, coldly.

'How's your mother?'

'She's not missing you, if that's what you're thinking.'

Christian winced as though he had been physically wounded by his daughter's words. Around them, other conversations buzzed frantically, squeezing every valuable second out of the short time these visiting sessions provided. Christian wondered why his daughter did not buzz that way. 'No words of kindness?' he asked, in a voice he did not recognise as his own.

'What would you like me to say?' Nina asked.

'I don't know. Do you really hate me that much?'

'Honestly, I'm not sure. You're still my father, but I find it hard, sometimes, to think why that alone should be enough for me to love you.'

Christian lowered his head, drew his fingers into tight fists. Perhaps on the outside he might have used those fists to beat an admission of love from this girl. But not in here.

In here, where his daughter wore the red visitor's vest and the guards carried the keys, he had no power.

'I deserve that,' he said. 'I deserve your hatred for what I've put you through, but you know everything I did, I did because I love you.'

Nina laughed and her breath was like ice. 'You really believe that, don't you?'

'Don't you?'

'No. I think you did it because you thought you were losing control of me. This is what this whole thing has been about, with you, with Nathan. You all just wanted to control me.'

'Protect you, Nina. I wanted to protect you.'

'By beating me up? By forcing me to get rid of my baby?'

'You couldn't have looked after it by yourself.'

'Nathan would have helped. If I'd told him the truth, rather than listening to you. Nathan wasn't evil, he was just looking for something.' Bitter-sweet memories cycled through her mind. 'I think I might have been that something. We could have been a family. I could have filled in the bit that was missing.'

'Listen to yourself, Nina. You're talking about the most selfish man I've ever known. He didn't care about you. He didn't want you.'

'That's where you're wrong. He did.'

Christian shook his head, his resolve hardening into anger. 'He told me, the day before I shot him. He said you wanted to be with him and he wouldn't let you get closer. He pushed you away.'

'He said that?' Nina's frozen smile grew distant. 'I suppose that's what he thought. Or maybe he just didn't want to let other people know what I was truly running from when I moved to London.'

'What are you talking about?'

'He pushed me away to protect me.' There was triumph in her tone. 'He wouldn't stay with me because he knew what you would do to me.'

'But. . .' Christian hesitated. 'No. That can't be right.'

'He was frightened you might kill me if he allowed himself to love me.'

'He never said anything like that to me.'

Nina rose and the guards at the door turned to watch her interestedly. 'Where did you think you were going at the station that day?'

'I asked him not to tell me.'

'You were going to London. He'd got my address from Lampar and he was coming to see me.' She slammed a clenched fist to her chest.

'He was coming to be with me and you shot him. You killed him and you think you did that for me?'

One of the guards manoeuvred through the tables and placed a hand on Nina's shoulder. 'Miss,' he whispered. 'I have to ask you to sit down or leave.'

Nina shrugged the guard's hand away and caught Christian in a stony gaze. 'It's okay,' she said. 'I'm leaving. There's nothing here for me anymore.'

Christian's throat worked rapidly, a jumble of thoughts and emotions wedged hopelessly behind his clenched teeth. His wide eyes were smeared and watery.

'Goodbye,' Nina said.

'I never. . .' Christian tried, but the words were useless, barely coherent. 'I didn't realise. He never said he. . .'

Nina shook her head. 'He shouldn't have had to.'

'I didn't know. I thought I was helping. You're just a kid. Sometimes kids go off the rails and need guidance. I only ever thought of you.'

Nina turned to the guard, who was hovering nervously. 'I'm ready to go,' she said.

Christian looked up. 'What are you going to do now?'

The look of superiority that passed across Nina's face cut through him like a knife. 'I have a job.'

'Where?'

'Lampar's stables.'

'How?'

'Nathan organised it for me.'

Christian's brow ran to deep furrows of confusion. 'Will you come back?'

'Is there any reason why I should?'

'I suppose not.' He swallowed. 'Did you go to his funeral?'

'Yes.'

'What was it like?'

'It rained. Only a few people showed up.'

'I'm sorry.'

She paused, then a slow, knowing smile spread across her face, as if she was remembering something. 'It doesn't matter anyway, does it?'

'Why not?'

'Because he wasn't there either.' Her smile was malicious and sad in the same instance. 'You never had as much power over me as you thought you did. You could hit and punch, but my life was always my own.' She leaned in close, whispering defiantly under her breath. 'I kept the baby.'

'You. . ?'

She turned quickly, walked away. Never looked back.

In the car, she took a letter from her purse and unfolded it. Specks of rain exploded on her windscreen as the drops spiralled down from a grey sky.

The letter had arrived in the post the day after Nathan had been murdered. He had obviously written it just before leaving for the train station. It had been addressed to 'My Guiding Light, so that I might find my way back from the dark places'.

She read it, as she had read it a hundred times before, started up the car, and drove to Zypher Fields Stables. By the time she got there, the sun had appeared through a haze of buttery clouds. The smell of spring was in the air.

She got out of the car. On the horizon, seagulls bobbed and flapped in unison. There were horses on the gallops, one of them was Tiffany's Toast, a beast worth considerably more since Neil Jacobson had ridden her to victory as Ascot and got some black type in her.

'Come on then, Nathan,' Nina said. 'We have work to do.'

She placed a hand on her stomach, which was noticeably swelled beneath purposefully loose-fitting clothes.

She took deep breaths.

Eventually, she felt movement. The sun grew hotter.

Sometimes people needed a reason to come back to the living. Sometimes, just sometimes, they were never truly gone.